TRIGGER
TALK

Also published in Large Print
from G.K. Hall by Nelson Nye:

Mule Man
Trail of Lost Skulls
Red Sombrero
Born to Trouble
Riders By Night
Wild Horse Shorty
Gunman Gunman
Wide Coop
Horse Thieves
Wolftrap

Nelson Nye

TRIGGER TALK

G·K·Hall&Co.

Boston, Massachusetts

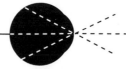

This Large Print Book carries the Seal of Approval of N.A.V.H.

Copyright © 1942 by Nelson Nye.
Copyright © renewed 1969.

Published in Large Print by arrangement with
Nelson Nye.

G.K. Hall Large Print Book Series.

Printed on acid free paper in the
United States of America.

Set in 16 pt. Plantin.

Library of Congress Cataloging-in-Publication Data

Nye, Nelson C. (Nelson Coral), 1907–
    Trigger talk / Nelson Nye.
        p. cm. — (G.K. Hall large print book series)
    (Nightingale series)
        ISBN 0-8161-5631-X (acid-free)
        1. Large type books.   I. Title.
    [PS3527.Y33T75 1993]
    813'.54—dc20   92-30141

Chapter 1

It was the day of the Big Blow, and every possible thing that might drift loose had been nailed down in Galeyville. Through the San Simon Pass the gale was howling like forty furies, and the lashing gusts that shrieked through the town were like lost souls sprung out of hell, when a man rode in on a sway backed horse whose ears were laying flat as pancakes.

He was a stranger, tall and gaunt in his miner's red shirt with 'dobe dollars sewn down the sleeve-sides. A Confederate cavalry sash was a clashing colour about his middle, half hidden by the flaps of a torn, mudstained vest that had once cost money and still was attractively spangled with flowers embroidered in gaudy-gay colours by somebody's needle. He wore baggy-kneed trousers, once buff, with a check pattern, whose ragged bottoms were carelessly stuffed into cavalry boots that were brush-clawed and dusty; but his spurs were of silver and bright as a knife-blade—bright as the look of his brash flashing stare.

He was a yellow-haired man with a small yellow moustache astride his top lip, and the rest of his face badly in need of a shave. Red dust made a film across his lean cheeks; but he had white teeth—as seen by his smile, and his name, he said, was Misery Jones.

"Well, by the Eternal, 'tis misery ye'll have if you don't get that dang bronc out of my bar!" Nick Babcock shouted, untying his apron.

The stranger's pale brows rose up two full inches.

"An' what's the matter with this horse, anyway?"

"Do you call that thing a *horse?*" asked a big, powerful fellow with twinkling black eyes.

Misery Jones shoved back his battered felt hat and scratched his head. With a quizzical smile he said:

"Well, I dunno . . . I thought 'twas a horse when I stole 'im."

"Don't make no diff'rence what you call him," growled Babcock. "Get him outa here an' get him out quick!"

Jones' blue stare went over Nick Babcock without much favour.

"I wouldn't put even a seam-squirrel out in a wind like this," he said mildly. "I'm surprised you've the heart to ask it."

"Aghr-r!" Nick Babcock, rolling his sleeves, advanced with a scowl. "Are you puttin' him out or ain't ye?"

"No!" blared Misery flatly; and Nick Babcock stopped in his tracks.

But he found nothing of threat in the stranger's look. He beckoned a couple of bouncers. "Get that carrion outa here quick!" And he strode towards Jones to help them.

"Now look," said the stranger patiently, hooking one knee around his saddle-horn. "I'm a peaceful jasper—if I'm left alone. When I ain't I'm a holy terror!"

He leaned and shook an admonitory finger under Nick Babcock's nose.

"If you aim to continue business in this stand, suh, you'd better leave my horse plumb alone."

" 'Cause you'll do what?" sneered Babcock.

"Live an' learn," Jones said, and shrugged broad shoulders philosophically. "It won't be no loss o' mine. But remember," he added sternly, *"you been warned."*

Now Galeyville was Curly Bill's stronghold, a boom silver camp and owl-hooter hang-out; and Babcock's place was the toughest in town—notorious for its frequent brawls, for its rotten booze and loose women. It had a name to live up to, and so had Nick; and, besides all this, the place was packed with miners, cowpokes and stage-boot robbers, all watching with grins and filling the air with their free advice.

Nick Babcock, scowling, gave the nod to his men, and they started, all three, for the stranger.

Jones never moved till the first big bruiser put a hand on his horse. And then all hell tore loose, seemed like. The stranger's left boot came up in an arc. It stopped hard against the big bouncer's jaw, and the man went down like a tent pole. Jones' quirt, butt first, made a centre-fire hit between the next man's eyes; and *he* lost all interest pronto.

Nick Babcock went stock still in his tracks, and surprise dropped his jaw wide open. Then he gnashed his teeth and said: "By Gawd—"

That far he got, and no farther. A gun made a racket that drowned out all sound, and when it quit all the glass in Nick's place was in shards on the floor and the barkeep's eyes were like bugs on a stick and the customers' faces were white as birch bark.

No man had seen the stranger's quick draw; but they all saw the smoking gun in his hand—in his *left* hand, at that, for his right was stiff-held by his belt buckle, its fingers wrapped round his bronc's reins.

Nick Babcock swallowed painfully. It was evident he wanted to say something—the look of his cheeks proved that. But what *could* you say after such an exhibition? To speak might invite a lot more of it. The stranger's thin smile was a warning.

But so was the look in Nick Babcock's eye.

The black-haired man beside him spoke then.

"Never mind your mirrors, Nick—I'll pay for them an' gladly." He was moving toward the stranger when the stranger's gun-filled hand rose in a gentle gesture that stopped him like an anchor dropped.

"Does the horse," Jones said, "stay in here, Mister?"

Some of the boys whooped loudly.

Nick Babcock scowled and without reply stamped into a back room, slamming the door.

The black-haired man said, "Don't mind him—he's a great guy when you know him.

My name," he stated with a gold-toothed smile, "is Graham . . ."

"Glad to know you, suh," said Misery Jones, and replaced his gun in its holster. "Were you, by any chance, the Graham that was with Stonewall Jackson's—"

"Well, no," said the man, still smiling, "I hadn't that pleasure—more's the pity. The—"

"Mebbe you was the Graham that held the bridge for—"

"No," said Graham a bit hastily; "I wasn't in the War—that is, directly."

"Suh, I rode with Jeb Stuart," Jones answered proudly, and some of the crowd raised a cheer. The stranger's quick grin showed the flash of his teeth. "We gave the damn' Yanks a run fo' theah money," he assured them; and flushed when he saw Graham's hand. "I'll have to shake with my left," he said; "my right flipper ain't much use any more—"

"Quite all right," Graham said. "If you've time for a drink, I'd feel honoured."

"Why not?" Jones said with alacrity; and swung down out of his saddle. "Just a second, suh!" He tied his bronc's reins to the bar rail, and followed Graham back to a table.

The barkeep hurried up with a bottle and a couple of none-too-clean glasses.

"This the best you got?" Graham said curtly.

The barkeep fidgeted.

Graham waved him away. "This is the worst rotgut in the Territory," he muttered; "but the rest of it's not much better. Your health," he said, lifting up his glass, "and may your finger never miss your trigger!"

The stranger guffawed and slapped Graham's back.

"No danger o' that," he chuckled, and put his glass down hurriedly while he coughed and strangled and spluttered. He looked at Graham with tears in his eyes and owlishly stared at Graham's empty glass. "By grab! You've sure got a gullet!"

The black-haired man flashed his gold-toothed smile.

"It's all in what you're used to," he shrugged. Then he leaned forward confidentially. "How would you like a job, Mister Jones? A *good* job that'll pay you well and mebbe work into a better one."

"Hold on a bit now. What *kind* of a job?" asked the man who called himself "Misery." "I'm hard up, I'll own; but I'm still particular. I won't rob widders or foreclose a mortgage—"

"Oh, it's nothing like that," Graham said airily. "It's a cow job I'm offerin'—"

"Been a long time since I punched any cattle," Jones frowned. "An' besides, there's my bum paw to—"

"It's a range boss that I'm looking for. A man who's quick with a gun."

Jones sat back to peer at him.

"I dunno . . . Quick with a gun, eh? Who you wantin' rubbed out, Mister Graham, suh?"

"Now, now—you're getting the wrong slant, pardner. An' don't go putting words in my mouth. It's not a rub-out I'm hiring you for. Call it rather a hint, or a put-out."

Graham met his look straight. Then he lowered his voice.

"It's like this: I got a ranch down along the San Simon. For the last couple of years the spread's been a pure loss. I put tenants on it, understand, an' they've turned out to be the most shiftless trash that I've ever yet had any dealings with. Why," he said, "they won't even pay me my lease money; an' I can't get 'em off the place!"

"Can't get 'em off?"

"They defy me," Graham sighed. "And the law's gone to hell in this country."

Jones rubbed a hand across his bristly jowls.

"An' you'd like me to put 'em off for you?"

"That's the ticket. No rough stuff if you can avoid it. But I want them moved out at any cost. And the ranny that moves 'em gets a range boss's job—"

"Suh," Jones said, "it's a bargain!"

Chapter 2

The wind had dropped, and heat-haze hung like a blue-grey smoke boiling against the footslopes of the distant Empire Mountains when Jones rode out of Galeyville at three by the slant of his shadow. The mauve crags of the Santa Ritas were lost in the storm, but here in the Cherrycows the sun was hotter than hell's backlog and the towering rocks shone bright as jet where the sunlight smashed from their sides.

In the San Simon Pass he pulled up to let his decrepit old horse catch its breath, and to look out over the countryside. You never could tell in this kind of region what might loom around the next yonder curve—particularly now, when carpet-baggers were a blight on the land. In the last few months Misery Jones had found it well to be prepared.

But he laughed to himself as he headed down the long sweeping slopes toward the spread of the San Simon Valley, for life after all was very good, and he was disposed to eye it more genially now that he'd a good feed under his belt and some work to keep his mind occupied.

Mister Graham had given him explicit directions for finding the Broken Bow, the ranch held down by the poor white trash who refused to cough up their lease money.

Misery Jones was in no doubt of the way and was quite content to ride leisurely while his glance roved approvingly around him. A fine large country, he thought it—a regular cowman's paradise. The long waving grasses gently brushed his stirrups and the soft callings of the sleepy mockers reminded him of Texas, and his mood at once turned nostalgic for the home he'd left behind.

And so he rode for a while and then heaved up a sigh, for the hallowed timbers that had known his youth were gone, destroyed by the Yankee infantry. He had gone back after Lee's surrender and found the place in ashes. Some few of his neighbours had been there, clinging on, and with many headshakes they had told him the news—how his mother had died three years before; how his father, discouraged and in poor health, had sold out to their former stable boss who was in high favour with the Yanks.

None had known where the old man went; but some had thought Arizona had lured him with its chance of free land and no taxes. But he'd well-nigh combed the country, seemed like, and he had not even had word of him—unless you counted the windy tale the horse-hunter had spun that he'd met at the Horsehead Crossing.

On the Pecos that had been, over yonder in New Mex—a wild and lawless region if he'd ever come across one. And he had known foul places, Jones mused—camps like Shakespeare, Tombstone, San Saba and others. But the man at Horsehead Crossing had claimed there were some Fenners over here in the Cherrycows: a crippled old man and his son, a high-stomached young squirt called "Dude", who by the barest chance might, Jones Fenner thought, be his young kid brother, Johnny.

At any rate he was here now and he'd certainly have his look, just as soon as he got this present chore done. For it might be them, sure enough. The gods were plainly smiling now, as witness this job for Bill Graham.

It had sure come in the nick of time, for he hadn't the price of a meal to his name unless he sold off his pistols. And Graham was a man a ranny could work for—handsome, soft-spoken—a regular gent, and bitterly being imposed on by a bunch of damn Yankee trash. Which was the way things went in this day of our Lord with beggars on horseback and quality hoofing.

Jones shook his head and looked around.

The rutted road here ran straight ahead between tall ranks of high-topped pines, with the sun's bright disk baking up a rank and resinous smell from them that was nectar to Misery Jones' soul. Cowbirds whirled in and out of their branches and abruptly departed *en masse* towards the south, and Jones' pale glance squeezed narrow.

He was not surprised when shortly afterwards a horseman jogged his fine bronc from the trees and stopped in the rutted trail. For this was a page torn out of a book Misery Jones knew line by line. The man stared around at him casually and sat waiting for him to come up.

The man's left hand came off his pommel in the Indian sign for peace; so Jones said, "Howdy," and looked him over with the care of considerable experience.

He was a black-haired fellow with laughing black eyes that yet had a quick questing in them. He wore cotton trousers of a tattle-tale grey with a green sash whipped around his belly and a yellow sombrero chinstrapped to his head. He was plainly a Mex, and a deep-seated crease on his nose was the mark of somebody's gun barrel—an old scar that, but potent with warning to a man of Jones Fenner's experience.

"You got tobacco?"

The man smiled as he said it, and Misery tossed over his sack. The Mex wrapped his reins around the saddle-horn and hooked a knee over them while he twisted Jones' Durham in a corn husk brought from his pocket.

"You got match?"

Misery gave him a match, brightly watchful. The fellow pulled smoke into his lungs and gave Jones back his tobacco sack, and sat awhile regarding him.

"You look for job?" he said at last; and Misery shook his head.

"My name Petralgo," the Mexican said; "Petro Petralgo."

"Right nice name," conceded Jones politely.

Petralgo's smile was a quick white flash, and he nodded his head.

"Very nice," he said. "You come from Galeyville—no?"

"What about it?"

Petralgo's eyes showed an ironic amusement. But he only shrugged and wheeled out of the road.

"I'm obliged," he said, "for tobacco."

"Hold on," Jones called; but the man was gone, fading swiftly away through the trees.

"Another durn stick-up," Misery muttered, peering after him. "The whole dang country's full of 'em—stick-ups an' carpetbaggers." He looked down at himself then and chuckled. "He didn't need no opera glass to tell him *I*'d be poor pickin's."

The late afternoon was drawing to a close and evening shadows were bluely crowding the range when he got his first look at the Broken Bow, the place Graham had leased to the white trash. It was down in a platter-shaped hollow but a stone's throw from the San Simon, as fine-looking a spread as a gent could ask for, and trim as a filly's shoulder.

Water made a pale white streak beyond the outfit's buildings, and the squat adobe ranch-house looked solid as a fort. Built for use beyond all doubt, with rugged outbuildings and pole corrals made of hand-hewn, solid timbers.

The cook had just stepped out of his shanty to give the call to supper, and he paused before he beat his pan to give Misery Jones the once-over. Three or four punchers strolling up from the corrals likewise gave him jaundiced stares. It wasn't their staring, but the way they did it. Jones felt about as welcome as a skunk at a parlour social.

And then Jones pulled his horse up suddenly and loosed a great shout at the man on the house veranda.

It was his *Dad!* By all that was holy, it was old Joe Fenner!

Misery sent his horse across the yard with a sudden quick jab of the spurs.

"Suh" he cried, grinning widely, "heah's yo' black-sheep son come home again!" and piled down out of the saddle.

But at the veranda's edge he stopped, his smile fading, for the man on the porch hadn't moved. No recognition brightened his face. It was as stern and cold as a well chain.

A younger man stepped out of the house and stared at Jones Fenner uncharitably.

"Who's this," he said, "and what's he want?" And without waiting for an answer, he said to Jones, "We've got no jobs for range bums!"

Jones stared. This arrogant fellow wore a stock at his throat and pearl-grey leg-clutching trousers. His coat was a brilliant bottle-green, and fine lace showed at his wrists. A tall beaver hat graced his shapely head, and his lips were curled back in a sneer. But there was no mistake—it was Jones' brother Johnny, and the man in the rocker was Jones' father.

Misery blinked, passed a hand across his eyes and shook his head with a bewildered smile.

"Sure you're funnin' me—you know me, don't you, Johnny? Your old busted flush of a brother—"

"I have no brother," John Fenner said; and Misery looked at his father.

But the old man shook his grizzled head. He picked up a cane off the porch planks and lifted himself to his feet.

"I don't know who you are, my boy, nor what kind of game you're playing. But 'twill do you no good, whatever it is."

Then John Fenner said:

"So be off with you. We've no place here for a range tramp." He started forward threateningly.

Misery gave him no heed. With brows drawn down, he was eyeing his father amazedly.

"But, *suh!*" he protested, "have you plumb forgotten your oldest boy, Jones? Don't you remember—he went to the War—"

"Aye—and died there. God rest his brave soul," the old man said.

"Died, hell!"

"If it was your intention to pass yourself off for my son who is dead, you would best have first learned my son's habits. My son," Joe Fenner said sternly, "never used the Lord's name in vain—no oath ever crossed his lips!"

"One's crossin' 'em *now,*" Jones muttered grimly. "I'll get to the bottom of this, by grab—"

"Don't fash yourself, stranger—and you can save your wild boasts," Joe Fenner cut in with a sneer. "We've the Government's own word for it. Jones Fenner was killed in action."

Misery stared, and his heart went sick inside him. So that was it! The mystery was solved. They had the Government paper, a formal notice of his death, and they would not go behind it. They had given him up for dead.

He could see now how shock and grief had aged his father—it was there in his stooping old shoulders, in his cane, in the silver that frosted his hair. And his brother—this insolent cub with his arrogant sneers, his fine lace and high beaver hat!—it was plain *he* had no wish to bring a dead brother to life!

Misery eyed them stiffly, heartsick and shaken, and finally shook his head.

"Well—all right," he said. "I guess that's proof. Could you give me some work—a rider's job, mebbe? I could earn my keep, I reckon."

The old man was fixing to speak, looked like, but young John Fenner cut in ahead.

"We've all the hands we need right now, and we've no grub to waste on a range bum. Try Galeyville—the town's full of tramps; another one'll never be noticed."

"Look," Misery said with a lifted temper, "I'm a little tired of that 'tramp' stuff. The Fenners have fallen on hard times all right, when they turn a hungry man from the door."

His brightened glance flicked to his father and he saw the old man hesitate; but it was plain John Fenner was bossing things now. Misery saw him wheel green-coated shoulders round, and his raised voice sailed across the yard:

"Hawswell!"

Misery saw a burly man detach himself from the watching group by the mess shack door. He came trotting across at a truculent stride; a bully-puss man with a tough-hombre manner that did not sit well on Jones' stomach.

"What'll yuh hev?" this buck said to John Fenner; and Misery's brother said coldly:

"Put this scum off Broken Bow Ranch!"

The Fenner range boss leered at Jones; but Misery's glance was hard-shoved at John Fenner, and there was a lash of flame in his cold pale stare.

"The Good Book's got a word for you—"

"C'mon," growled Hawswell. "Hop it!"

But Jones gave the man no slightest attention. All his mind was on his dandified brother. It had been four years since they'd seen each other, yet he was certain John Fenner knew him; and it was as bitterly certain the man had no intention of admitting their relationship, come what might.

But Jones was determined to have one last try.

"John—"

That far he got, and that far only. Something hard and swift came down on his head, and the world was blanked out by a haze of stars.

Chapter 3

When his mind came back to realities night had fallen and he was alone in the dust of a road with a cold wind flapping his shirt, with his head feeling as if a mule had kicked it, and with a body so bruised it hurt him to move. But he knew he could not stay in the road; some larruping horseman might tramp him to death. With a groan he got his good hand under him, braced it and, somehow, managed to get to his knees; and that way, like a crippled dog, he crawled to the side and collapsed again.

How long he lay there he never knew; but, at last awake, he roused himself and found that, with a deal of pain, he could stand up. He braced himself against a tree and with his good hand felt himself over. He was not so badly off as his aches had prophesied; there were no broken bones at any rate. But he was badly in need of a bed, sure enough; they must have pounded the daylight out of him.

He stared morosely around for his horse, but the critter wasn't with him—they had kept it probably, or maybe shot it. And his hat was gone, and his shirt torn to hell, and his pistol was gone from his holster. Oh, they'd done him up proud, he thought bitterly.

He had no idea where he was. Probably on the Galeyville road. They'd brought him out here and dumped him—as they'd dump a sack of old rubbish.

He lifted a hand to scratch at his head and found his hair matted with blood. *That* would have been Hawswell, the range boss; he must have batted him down with a gun barrel.

He sighed again and turned a painful look about, but saw no sign of light anywhere There seemed nothing for it but to get on the move; he couldn't stand there all night or he'd freeze.

So, doggedly, he commenced walking, following the course of the road. It was bound to take him some place, if he could manage to keep going that long.

It seemed as if he'd tramped for centuries before at last, away off somewhere to the left, he saw the faint shine of a lamp. It was like a beacon with its held-out hope of sanctuary; and he stumbled towards it, muttering.

He could have reached it easily if it had only stood still; but it wouldn't. It kept dancing away just beyond his reach, and bitterly he cursed it. But he kept on going, stumbling, falling—sometimes crawling; for it wasn't Jones' way to quit.

Finally, ages later, he must have somehow caught up with it, for he heard a girl say clearly, "Why—why, Dad! It's a man!"

It was the last thing he heard for a long time.

Misery was running a few degrees of fever, so it seems more or less understandable that his next clear recollection was of a copper-haired angel with fine cool hands who lugged around a ten-gallon jug which she insisted that he sample every time she came within gunshot of him. Not that he was on the wagon or put up any fuss about it. There was more kick in it to the cubic gulp than could be found in a case of dynamite; and every time he took a swig he felt six inches taller.

But there finally came a time when, opening his eyes, he saw things in their proper light. He was in a cabin some place, and flat on his back in a bunk. A redheaded girl sat near its foot busily darning somebody's socks. An occupation totally unsuited to her, Misery thought.

She looked up and found him watching her, and her rosy lips parted in a radiant smile that made Misery catch his breath.

"Uh—er—gosh!" he stammered. "You must be the girl with the jug!"

"Jug?"

There was a question in her look, and tiny lines of puzzlement sprang up between her dark eyes.

"Sure—don't you remember? You kep' bringin' it 'round an' making me drink—"

"Oh! Yes," she said. "Did you like it?"

Misery nodded. "Where is this; an' how long've I been heah anyhow?"

"Now you just get to sleep," she said, "and I'll tell you all about it, later."

Misery said:

"I reckon, ma'am, I'm sure bound to oblige you. Er—I'm Misery Jones . . ."

She looked at him shyly.

"I'm Taisy Crawford—and now you must go to sleep, please."

Much later, when he woke again, there was a man in the cabin with them, a tall man with a clean-shaven face that was as pale as John Fenner's stock. He was dressed in sober black store clothes that were neat, although rather threadbare. He seemed to be studying Misery, and then he said abruptly:

"How're you feeling, son?"

"Suh, I'm feelin' like gettin' up," Misery answered, and scowled around for the girl.

His face lighted up when he saw her. She was putting food on a plain slab table; and the tantalizing aroma of it made Misery aware he was starving.

"Like getting up, eh?" The tall man smiled. "You'll do better to stay in bed a bit longer—you were in pretty bad shape when we found you—"

"I'm feelin' a mighty sight better now—"

"Well, you stay in bed for the rest of the day, and tomorrow we'll let you get up," the man said.

Then Taisy came over and, colouring gently, said, "Mister Jones, this is my father, Morgan Crawford."

"I'm glad to meet up with you, suh," Misery said, and Crawford came over and shook his hand—the left one, because his bum paw was under the blanket.

Taisy came over then with a steaming bowl

of some kind of broth which Misery swallowed very slowly in order to keep her there as long as he could.

She sure was mighty fine calico—neat as a new pin, and so pretty and sweet that bee trees were gall alongside her. She had soft, curved lips that were red as cherries and teeth with the lustre of pearls. There was the glint of copper in her high-massed hair, and her eyes were soft wells in the twilight. She was the best looking filly he had ever seen, and quality marked every line of her. She was like a dream, and he wished he might never wake up.

She discovered him watching her, and a rosy colour stole over her cheeks and a shy smile brought out her dimples and caused her father to clear his throat.

"It might," he observed, "be a good idea, Taisy, if we let Mister Jones get to sleep for a while."

Misery got up the next morning. Morgan Crawford appeared a bit dubious about the advisability of it, but Misery took on so that he finally relented and helped him on with his clothes. Taisy, Crawford said in reply to Jones' enquiry, was out milking the cows.

"When she gets through fussing 'round with her hens, she'll come in and get you some breakfast."

"Suh," Jones said, "I sure hate to put you all to so much trouble."

"That's quite all right. No trouble at all. I've a razor here if you'd like to clean up—but take it easy. You don't want to overdo things now—"

"Shucks," Misery grinned, "I'm fit as a fiddle. How long have I been heah anyway?"

"Four days. Head bothering you any?"

"Nary a bother."

"That was a pretty bad gash," Crawford told him. "Looked like you'd been pistol-whipped."

"Yeah—wounds sure are misleadin', ain't they? You own this spread?"

"We're homesteading here."

"Surprised some cow outfit ain't moved you," Jones said, and saw the quick glint in the tall man's stare as he returned with a wash pan and razor. He set them down on the table alongside a towel and a wash cloth. "About how far," Jones asked him, "are we from the Fenner place?"

Morgan Crawford's lips went a little tight and he shot Misery a peculiar stare. But he said readily enough:

"About five miles. They're north of us—towards San Simon. Do you know the Fenners?"

Misery scowled.

"I'm acquainted with them."

Crawford's grey brows rose at his tone, but he didn't ask any questions.

Misery hitched his chair closer to the table and commenced scraping off his whiskers. When Taisy came in some twenty minutes later she found him looking more presentable. She gave him a smile and a pleasant "Good morning," and Misery's pulse picked up amazingly.

"I guess you're pretty hungry," she said, and Misery got up gallantly.

"Ma'am," he grinned, "I could eat a bear!"

"A couple pieces of toast and a little tea—" Crawford began, and chuckled at the dour expression of his guest. "Well, maybe a couple of boiled eggs then—"

"An' anything else you can spare," Misery said. "I got a long ways to travel—"

"You'll be doing no travelling today, young fellow. You'll have to laze around a couple of days before you'll be fit to do any walking—"

"Who said anyth—Oh! Yeah—that's

right. How-somever, I've got a horse—if he ain't died of old age since I saw him last. The Fenners," explained Misery carefully, "have been taking care of it for me. If you'll just lend me a horse to get to their ranch—"

"I may be having some business over that way," Crawford mentioned. "If you'd like I could—"

"That's sure obligin' of you, suh, but I expect I better get the nag personal," Misery said, and the dark scowl he showed put an end to their talk for the moment.

After he had eaten, Misery pushed back his chair and rolled up a smoke.

"I expect," he said, "you been doin' considerable wonderin' about me—an' I ain't blamin' you a bit. The plain fact is—"

"Just a moment, son," Morgan Crawford said. "There's really no call for you—"

"I reckon not," Misery grumbled; "but I'd rather you'd hear it from me than some others, an' there'll be plenty to peddle the story. Seems like range tramps ain't wanted 'round that Broken Bow outfit. They got a way with such gentry—as they took the trouble to show me. What them polecats overlooked was that I might take some trouble *myself* 'fore I quit."

"Are you telling us," Taisy cried, "it was the Fenners who—who—"

"I ain't namin' no names," Misery muttered; "but there'll be a hereafter fo' three or fo' gents. You watch my smoke an' get educated!"

"Tck, tck, tck," clucked Crawford. "Nothing good will come out of that."

Taisy murmured reprovingly, "Two wrongs, Misery, can never make a right."

"Never mind," growled Misery. I'm peaceful as a pan o' milk so long as I'm treated Christian. But when a guy does me dirt, I pay him in kind—with plenty of compound interest!"

Morgan Crawford shook his head.

"You won't get far with the Fenners, my boy. The Broken Bow is one of the most powerful ranches in this Territory; and you might just as well go and shoot yourself as to have any Fenner for an enemy."

"Hoo, hoo!" jeered Misery; and suddenly scowled. "Do you think I'm a-scared of them tinhorns? By grab, I'll make them hard to catch—you wait! I'm a hetankarora from the Cantamount Sinks an' I don't take that stuff off *no*body!"

Taisy sighed, and her father shook his head glumly.

"There won't be any good come out of it," he said. "You'll get the worst of anything you start with the Broken Bow—"

"And, anyway," declared Taisy, "you're bound to admit they had some *cause* for distrusting you. You *did* look like a range tramp—"

"I thought you was my friend!"

"I am," Taisy said, with her chin up. "But I'm a friend of Dude Fenner's also, and I know Dude would not do a dishonest thing—"

"Oh, is that so?" Misery cried hotly.

Then he remembered that, after all, it was poor return for their kindness for him to shoot off his mouth in that manner. It was the Broken Bow crowd and a certain black-haired joker in Galeyville that his righteous wrath should fall on; and he put a quick rein on his temper, and flushed as he recalled all the work this girl must have gone to in washing, patching and ironing to get his clothes looking so neat. She'd even tallowed his boots up so that the scuffed places weren't so quickly noticed.

He said, "I beg yo' pardon, ma'am; I'm sure actin' up mighty ungrateful. Do you know," he asked her father, "of a person in Galeyville who goes by the name of Bill Graham?"

Morgan Crawford's pale face looked startled; and he flashed a quick look at his daughter. She, too, seemed to know that name; and Crawford said very gravely:

"I—ah—I trust he's not a friend of yours?"

"*Friend* ain't *my* name for him! He hired me to go to the Broken Bow—which he claimed was his ranch—an' put off a batch of poor white trash which he claimed wouldn't pay up their lease money!"

Morgan Crawford nodded.

"It sounds very like him," he said. "He's done that before. He's a bad man, son, and a mighty good fellow to steer clear of. He hasn't a penny tied up in that ranch; you may take my word—not one penny. He's an out-and-out crook, a horse thief and rustler—"

"Oh-ho! So he's trying to steal the place, is he?"

"Yes," Taisy said; "but Dude is too smart for him—"

"Dude?"

"Well, his right name," she said, "is John Fenner. His father owns the Broken Bow Ranch; but it's Dude that really runs it. He's a cowman from his boot-heels up. We're proud of him, aren't we, Father?"

"He seems to be quite a young gentleman—"

"Yes! And so considerate of other folks—particularly those less fortunate. Why, this was part of his range; and he wasn't at all put out when we came in and filed on it. He's always stopping 'round to see if we're comfortable, or if there's anything he can do for us. And poor Julie Flystrom—they're on Dude's range, too, over beyond the San Simon. Her father was a Union gunner, who got hurt at Shiloh and finally died. She brought her mother out here, and they're homesteading, too; only Julie does all the work, of course, because her mother has got some bronchial trouble and can't do anything at all, hardly. Why—"

"Yes," her father said, "Dude's been very good to them. But about this Graham person, Mister Jones; you want to keep well away from him. He's what they call 'bad medicine' out here. His right name's Brocius—Curly Bill Brocius. He's the outlaw the Earps ran out of Tombstone several months back."

"You mean to say," cried Misery, startled, "that this Graham pelican is 'Curly Bill,' the owl-hooter boss?"

Crawford nodded.

"A dead shot, they say, and the most notorious man in this country. He killed Marshal Fred White and a whole lot of others, and Wyatt Earp has sworn to get him if it takes the rest of his lifetime—"

"So that's Curly Bill," Misery muttered, amazed. "Why, the whole Southwest is talkin' about him. They hung one of his men in Shakespeare—some feller called Russian Bill—"

"That's the one," Crawford nodded. "My advice to you is to have no dealings with him—"

"I'll tend to him. When I've settled my score with these Broken Bow—"

"You're not! You won't!" cried Taisy fiercely. "I'll not have you fighting with Dude Fenner! It's all a misunderstanding! Dude—"

"I guess it was a 'misunderstanding' when that whoppy-jawed range boss of his—that Hawswell polecat—rapped his gun barrel across my head while I was talking with your fine Dude Fenner!"

"Mister Hawswell must have jumped to conclusions."

"Yeah!" Misery blared. "An' I'll jump *him!* He'll think a sea-snake's got him! I'm peaceful as a pinkbow kitten so long's I'm treated right; but when I'm taken advantage of—watch out!"

"That's just being hateful," Taisy said scornfully. "And it's not right to accuse Dude—"

"Right!" thundered Misery. "Where do you get that 'right' stuff? If someone slapped one side of your face, I guess you'd turn the other side 'round so they could take a poke at that, eh?"

"I think you're terrible!" Taisy said; and slammed the door shut behind her.

Misery Jones climbed out of his chair and scooped up his hat.

"I guess I know when I ain't wanted—"

"Now hold on, son," Morgan Crawford said, and put a quick hand on his arm. "No sense *you* going off half cocked just because Taisy's excited. Women don't look at things like men; a man relies on his eyes and judgment—a woman just follows her heart. I'm not saying you're right or you're wrong; but you've got to admit Dude's a handsome young devil, and looks mean a lot to a woman. He's been seeing quite a bit of Taisy—seems to go out of his way to drop by here; and, naturally, Taisy's been flattered by it. You don't want to judge her too harshly, son. The cares of the world have never comedown on her real hard till just here of late—"

"Mebbe not," Misery growled; "but *you* ought to know better—"

"And perhaps I do," remarked Crawford gravely. "But I've not knocked 'round this world fifty years without picking up a few facts. You can't handle women like you'd handle a horse. You've got to use tact—tact and patience."

He studied Jones a moment.

"Supposing you just sit down for a bit and tell me all about this business."

Still glowering, with doubt and resentment still jabbing him, Misery flopped himself down in a chair. But he said nothing about his name being Fenner; he confined himself exclusively to the physical aspects of the situation. He said:

"I've told you how it was, suh. This Graham galoot hired me on to ride out to this Broken Bow spread and get him shut of some tenants which, he said, wouldn't cough up their lease money. Not suspecting nothing, I was standing there talking with young Fenner when this cur-dog, Hawswell, steps up behind an' belts me down with his sixgun."

"Still, you can't wholly blame him,"

Crawford murmured reflectively. "You show up looking like a range tramp and order the Fenners off their ranch—"

"It hadn't got that far when Hawswell took chips. I was askin' for a job—"

"What kind of play was that?"

"Well," Misery said, "I had my reasons."

Then, under Crawford's stare, he stirred in his chair uncomfortably. He hadn't figured to say anything about being personally related to the Fenners, but it did look more or less thin as things stood to expect Crawford to put much stock in him. So, to bolster his story, he said the first thing that popped into his head.

"I don't want this to go any further—don't want you to even tell Taisy; but it happens I'm kind of a poor relation to them Fenners. So when I see who it was running the Broken Bow outfit, my errand kind of slipped my mind—most particular when they stood out to have no truck with me, wouldn't recognize me even—an' called me a plain damn' range tramp. So pretty quick I quit jawin' an' says, 'How about a job?' An' that was when Hawswell slugged me."

Morgan Crawford, with one bony hip hooked over the table, slouched for a considerable while in thought. Another T.B.,

Misery figured, who'd come trekking down here for his health. His pale, sunken cheeks and parchment hands, his frail, hollowed chest and stooping shoulders, all spoke of the Eastern office man who had picked up the "White Man's Plague".

Then, finally, Crawford roused himself. He swept a searching glance across Misery's face.

"Well, I'll tell you, Jones. What you've said pretty well confirms the impression I'd gathered of Dude Fenner. The old man seems a pretty square sort, but it's young Dude rules that outfit. He's a pretty slick pumpkin, from all I've seen—"

"Now, don't you jump at conclusions, Mister Crawford, suh. After all, I *did* look pretty much like a tramp—"

"But you were related to Dude; and, while the old man doesn't see too good, there's nothing wrong with Dude's eyesight. He chose to let on he didn't know you, but I venture to guess if you'd worn the habiliments of prosperity Dude would have received you with open arms. He's the kind that can trim his sails to the wind very quick—and to any wind that blows."

"Now it's all right for *me* to knock my relatives—"

"But you don't want other folks doing it."
Crawford smiled. "That's understandable
enough, and does you credit. But a goose
is a goose in any tongue—Just what do you
propose to do?"

"I dunno . . . ." Jones scowled. "But there
ain't no one can shovel on me without gettin'
dung throwed back at 'em. I'm sure goin'
after that Curly Bill's hide—"

"You best leave him for the Earps, boy.
He's a pretty tough monkey—"

"An' I ain't no man to—"

"It's your funeral," Crawford nodded;
"but you'd best keep in mind what I've told
you. If you go along back to Galeyville you'll
be shoving your head in the lion's mouth—"

"Shucks, I'll eat the durn critter, hoofs,
hide an' all! He's a fish-bellied shorthorn,
an', by grab, I'll prove it!"

Misery jumped to his feet and shook a
quick look round the room.

"Where the Sam Hill is my pistol?"

"Right over there on the sideboard—"

"Not that! I'm talkin' about my—Hell's
whiplash!" Misery grumbled. "I've just re-
collected! I done lost her over to Fenners'."

Crawford looked bewildered.

"Lost who?"

"My holster gun!"

Crawford's look still seemed a little muddled. "I can't see but what one gun's as good as another—"

"You don't understand. I can't go up against a guy like Bill Graham without a gun in my holster—"

"What's the matter with that pearl-handled—?"

But Misery was frowningly pacing the room. He appeared so flustered and irreconcilable that Crawford said, "Here—will this help you out?" and brought forth a six-shooter from the table drawer.

"Suh," Misery said; and then the quick light faded out of his stare. "Nope, I couldn't take it, suh. You've got to think of yo' own protection. With all these varmints that's ridin' the hills, a man can't risk goin' 'round unarmed. I'll just have to make out—"

"Nonsense," Crawford declaimed. "I don't need a gun any more than a rabbit. Here—take it. If you're set on tackling Curly Bill, what you *really* need is a cannon."

"Shucks," Misery said. "I'll sure fix his clock."

Then, just as he was sliding the proffered six-gun in the leather, he looked up to find Taisy watching from the doorway.

"I'm ashamed of you, Father!" she burst

out angrily. "After all Dude Fenner has done for us! To give your best gun to his enemy! How can you *be* so thoughtless?" Then she flashed Misery Jones a look of cold scorn. "I shall tell Dude he'd better watch out for you!"

But Misery laughed as he reached for his hat.

"You won't have to," he said. "The Dude knows it!"

Chapter 4

In Crawford's borrowed stiff hat and astride Crawford's horse, Misery Jones, in the shank of that same afternoon, re-appeared at the Fenner headquarters.

It would not be strictly true to describe his reception as "rousing"—but it did have its elements of drama. He was met at the gate by the burly boss, Hawswell, whose manner was not over-cordial.

"What're *you* doin' here?" Hawswell scowled, and clamped a quick hand on his gun butt.

"Never mind the artillery," Misery said mildly, "I've just come huntin' my horse."

"Then you can just turn around an' hunt

somewhere else," snapped Hawswell, belligerence bright in his stare. "Does this place look like a glue factory?"

"Aw—he wasn't *that* bad," declared Misery. "He might of had a few spavins an' he was a little mite swaybacked, but—"

"Go on!" growled the range boss menacingly. "I got no time to jaw with you— I'm s'prised you got the gall t' come back here!"

"Oh, I got plenty of gall, all right. What I'm lookin' for now is my horse—"

"Well, he ain't around here. Go on—hop it!"

"Don't rush me, friend," Jones told him coldly. "If he ain't here—why, then that settles it. But I *lost* a horse here, an' I'm not pullin' out till you fork over another in place of him."

The range boss started to pull his gun, but he stopped the movement very suddenly. And his face went pale as a piece of wet bread and he fell back half a step, goggling—and with mighty good reason. For though Jones' right hand still rested on his saddle-horn holding his reins, a short-barrelled gun had appeared in his left, and its muzzle gaped large, black and ugly.

"Just stand right there an' hold steady,"

Jones bade. "Ever had much experience yo-delling?"

"Y-yodelling?"

"Ain't nothin' wrong with your hearin'. Try a yodel now—open your face right up, boy."

The foreman's face got extremely red, but he didn't release any yodels. He looked more as if he were bent on murder—except that he didn't bend, even a fraction. He stood right still like a petrified tree; and Misery said coaxingly:

"Come on, sport. Pull a good deep breath in your lungs an' let go."

The foreman glowered, suddenly opened his mouth, and as suddenly—furiously—closed it.

"I ain't got all day," Jones drawled. "It'll begettin' grub time pretty quick, an' I aim to be a long ways from heah then. Liquidate yo' gastric juices an' fetch me out a quick yodel—"

"You go to hell!"

"Well, I may go there, but I won't go alone." Jones grinned and thumbed back the hammer of his short-barrelled gun.

Hawswell let out a frightened bleat.

"Not bad," Misery smiled, "for a starter. Now really open 'er up this time an' yowl for yo' hands to saddle up yo' bronc. You better, 'cause I'm gettin' right impatient."

The look of the range boss was something to remember; but he called for. the horse, and Jones saw a puncher grab up his rope. Then Hawswell snarled in a teeth crunching voice:

"By Gawd, you can't git away with this! I'll—"

"You'll shout, too, probably—after I'm gone," Misery chuckled. "But right now you're goin' to do like I tell you or I'll sure collect what you owe me. An' when I collect, I do it with compound interest."

He flicked a quick glance corralwards.

"They've got yo' bronc under saddle—tell one of 'em to fetch it over here. An' be *mighty careful*, Hawgswill."

It looked as if Hawswell were about to choke. His eyes were like knots on a stick. But he grunted out the order. And when a puncher brought a fine black saddler up to the gate, Misery said:

"Just have this lad write me out a bill o' sale, Hawgswill. I don't want to be mistook fo' no rustler."

The puncher couldn't see Jones' menacing gun, and he looked at his boss kind of startled.

Hawswell was startled, too; but, mostly, he was fit to be tied. And he had his mouth pulled back to curse, but he closed it without anything getting out but his breath, which was crossed between a sigh and a groan. Then, wickedly, he snarled at the cowboy:

"What the hell you waitin' on? Get a paper an' write that bill of sale, an' be goddam quick about it"

The startled puncher tore off to obey, and Jones gave the range boss a knowing wink.

"I can see you'd make a first-class soldier. By the way, where's John Fenner hidin' out these days?"

But Hawswell had his jaw clamped tight.

"Watch out," Misery said, "or you'll bust yo' nutcrackers, bucko. I bet yo' spit would blister a mule."

At about that time the puncher came up with Jones' bill of sale.

"Much obliged to you, suh," he drawled, carelessly thrusting it into his pocket. "You better go and help yo' friends hold up the bunk-house. This is a private confluence we're havin' here."

The cowboy shot a look at Hawswell; but Hawswell had cut his signal cord and wasn't saying yea or nay. Nor did he speak till the puncher got out of earshot. Then he raged:

"You think you're pretty damn smart, I reckon! Let me tell you somethin', Mister—"

"Aw—make a noise like a hoop an' roll away!" Misery scoffed, and contemptuously put his gun away. "You would-be badmen make me laugh—where I come from you wouldn't scare the kids! Hand me up the reins o' that black wreck now—"

"I'll see you in hell firstl" Hawswell gritted. His face was purple and flecks of foam edged the corners of his mouth; but Misery Jones just grinned his sour grin.

"Make haste, hombre, because your score with me figgers up like hell, an' when I tack my interest on there won't be nothin' left of you but what the paddy shot at."

Speechless, Hawswell handed up the reins. But the look of his eyes was ugly. It got uglier when Misery, flipping him a dollar, said:

"An' here's a cartwheel to bind the bargain—the nag ain't much better'n a crowbait, but he'll have to do till a decent one comes along."

He grinned widely down into Hawswell's black face.

"Well, *adios, amigo.*"

He tipped his hat derisively and, without looking back, rode off.

It was in a singularly pleased and expansive mood that, having left Crawford's horse at the cabin bright and early the next morning, Misery Jones rode back into Galeyville. He took in the sights with a cheerful smile and strode into Babcock's bar.

"Fill 'em up," he said. "Fill 'em up for the house."

The pasty-faced worm of a bartender fetched him a squint-eyed stare.

"Let's see the colour of your money, bucko."

Jones drew himself up straightly. "Are you aimin' to incinerate—"

"The rules of this place are cash in advance—"

"Then the rules are goin' to get broken. Don't forget," Misery grinned, "that what I did to your mirrors—I can do just as good by yo' bottles."

The bartender scowled like two pair at three tens, but Nick Babcock wasn't around, so, muttering, he commenced setting out glasses.

"C'mon, boys," Misery called to the crowd, "belly up an' get a snootful;" and the loungers waited no longer. Misery didn't drink himself. He said, "I'll take a cigar, Manuel."

The bartender cursed deep down in his throat.

"My name is Ralph—an' I'm no damn Mex—"

"I'm sure glad o' that; most Mexes are mighty nice people. Where's your pot-bellied boss?" Misery said; and the barman very nearly choked. He cast an appealing glance at the crowd, but the barflies were busy lapping up the free booze, and what few were listening were grinning.

Then the swing doors creaked open and Babcock came in with Curly Bill right on his boot-heels.

"H'are you, fella?" Misery Jones sang out; and Graham stopped short in his tracks.

"I thought I hired you for a job of work—"

"That's me—Yours Truly, M. Jones, suh."

"What are you doin' round here then?"

"Don't scowl," Jones said; "you'll git wrinkles. Don't you never use yo' eyes, Mister Graham? Then you sure ought to know what I'm doin' heah; I've done come after my money."

Curly Bill's black arrogant stare raked him over from boot-heels to headgear.

"I don't usually pay a man till he gets his work done—"

"Who says it ain't done?" Jones countered.

"Where's your proof?" Graham said with his stare gone narrow; and Nick Babcock snorted derisively.

"You better take yo' squint on out to the hitch rail an' give yo' eyes some more exercise. My horse is hitched right outside the do'—that black saddler that's packin' the Broken Bow brand."

With a puzzled scowl Curly Bill followed Babcock out. When they came back, Graham's scowl was more prominent.

"Where'd you get that bronc?"

"Why, I swapped with Hawgswill, the Broken Bow straw boss." Jones puffed his cigar complacently. "An' now that you've sampled the proof of the puddin', suppose you shell out, like prophesied."

"I ain't shellin' out till I know more about this," Graham muttered. "There's somethin' goddam queer about—"

"When I do a job of work for a guy I expect to get paid," blared Misery, turning ugly. "You better shell out an' shell damn quick or your heirs 'll start inheritin'!"

And, for the first time in his checkered career, Curly Bill found himself staring down a six-gun.

Chapter 5

To say Bill Graham was considerably surprised would be the wildest of understatements. He was the most amazed man this side of Red River—but he was one of the smartest, likewise. He concealed his feelings in a good-natured laugh; then said:

"By George, you're worth it! Where'd you learn to sling a gun like that? By George, I'm plumb tickled to know you!"

But Misery was no Johnny-Come-Lately to be undone by a show of good humour—or any other show, for that matter. If this Bill Graham was Curly Bill Brocius, he was the deadliest killer unhung—and no kind of hombre to stamp and shout *Boo!* at. Misery kept his gun trained square on Bill Graham's chest. He said:

"Count it on the bar, boy."

Curly Bill pulled out his wallet, but he took his time counting out the money, and every gent in Babcock's bar stood and watched with his jaws wide open.

"That's enough," Jones said abruptly. "Never mind the bonus—I'll collect for that on the next job."

Graham's eyes held a skeptical humour as he thrust his fat wallet back into his pocket.

"Fair enough," he said, scratching his back against the bar. "So you've really put them Fenners out, have you?"

"Out?" Misery grinned widely as he scooped up Graham's money and stuffed it inside his flowered vest. "What would you say if I told you them Fenners had burned your place flat to the ground?"

"What!" roared Curly Bill, and the whites of his eyes turned red as copper and his cheeks went black and wicked. "D'you mean to say—"

"Well, it ain't that bad," Jones admitted. "They ain't done more than sell out on you—but I'll tell you what I'll do. You treated me right when I came into this town lookin' down-an'-out as a range tramp; you thought I was broke an' you gave me a job. So this is what I'll do for you; I'll sell you back that Broken Bow spread for just what it cost—ten thousand."

Curly Bill's face was a mottled pink and every vein bulged on his forehead. He ran a trembling hand through the bush of black hair that showed beneath his white Stet hat, and his jowls went a jaundiced yellow.

"Sold out!" he gritted, and his black eyes bulged and he banged the bar in a passion. "Why, them—"

"Now, wait," Misery grinned. "You're dealin' with *me,* an' I've taken a look at the papers. You never owned so much as a corral post in that outfit—it was a good bluff, Bill, but it didn't work. So what are you goin' to do now? You goin' to pay me, or you goin' to tell your cattle-thief gang to try and rustle me out?"

Curly Bill eyed him, his glance bright and dangerous; then suddenly he grinned.

"By godfries, you re a cool one!" he grudgingly admitted. "Tellin' me to my face I never owned—"

"The land office records are mighty convincin'," Jones hinted. "But suit yo'self— I'd as lief have the ranch as the money."

"You never give ten thousand—"

"Well, no," Jones said, and chuckled. "I never give that much, for a fact; but I got to make a profit. I can't go buyin' up ranches an' then sell out fo' jest what I paid. How, much *will* you give for it?"

"I'll give you four thousand dollars—an' not a cent more!"

"By grab! You'd sell yo' gran'maw, wouldn't you? Four thousan' bucks for a spread worth more than double that! Why, it'd easy bring six at an auction!"

"It won't get to no auction," Graham smiled; and Misery Jones believed him.

"Well, I'll tell you," he said; "I'll split with you. Fork over five thousand an' my hold on it's yours—"

"Done," Graham snarled, and jerked out his wallet and heaped the bills up on the bar.

"Dunno's I ought to take that much paper—"

"What's the matter with it?"

"I don't reckon anything is—far as you're concerned. But I'd feel safer if 'twas in silver—"

"Do I look like a walkin' mint?" Graham glowered.

"Okey. I'll take a chance," Jones said, and put out a hand for the money.

"Not so fast," Graham purred. "Where's your bill of sale—or the deed? I ain't buyin' no pig in a poke—"

It was Jones' turn to scowl; and he did it.

"What do you take me for—a highway robber? You can go an' look at the records—"

"All right!" Jones growled. "The deal is off!" and started for the door.

Graham grabbed hold of his shoulder.

"Oh, no, you don't! I won't be put off! You stand right up to the bar there an' write me out a bill-o'sale an' slap your John-Henry on it!"

"That won't be legal—"

"Legal enough for me!" growled Graham. "Give 'im a paper an' pencil, Sligo—there! There you are! Hop at it!"

Misery holstered his six-shooter and scrawled a few words conveying to "William Graham" all the rights and interests of one "Misery Jones"—his heirs and assigns forever—in a property known as "Broken Bow Ranch." Then he flung down the pencil disgustedly.

"It won't hold water—"

"It'll hold all the water *I* want!" Graham grinned; and Jones stuffed the money in his pocket.

"You stick with me," Graham told him, "an' you can hitch your wagon to any damn star you fancy. We could go a long way together—"

"No, thanks," Misery scowled. "You're a sight too sudden for my speed. I know when I'm outclassed without havin' to consult no horoscope!" And he stamped out of Bab-cock's bar.

But once out of sight of Graham and his satellites, he gave vent to a hearty guffaw. He had taken Bill Graham clean down the pike, and right in the outlaw's own stronghold. "Jest wait till the news gets 'round," he chuckled; and headed for Shotwell's store, still laughing.

In Shotwell's Misery bought a new outfit, from cream Stet hat down to fancy Hyer boots; and he stuffed his pockets with cartridges for his guns and his new Sharps rifle.

He was crimping his ten-gallon Stet hat when he chanced to glance through a window. He paid his bill up in a hurry and made a bee-line for the door.

"Here—wait!" Shotwell called. "What about these old clothes—"

But Misery never even heard him. He was climbing into his saddle, hellbent, and his fastest was none too much hurry. For Hawswell, the Broken Bow range boss, had just stamped into Babcock's bar!

Chapter 6

No one had to tell Misery Jones what would happen if he didn't get out of town pronto.

He sent the big black up an alley and dashed across unmarked range, bent on getting into the yonder foothills in the shortest time he could manage. Curly Bill would howl for his scalp just as soon as he'd talked to Dude's foreman. He'd go hog-wild on the warpath; and sad would be one Misery Jones' fate if Curly Bill ever caught up with him!

There was some timber up there ahead and Misery slammed the black toward it. He felt no shame in using his spurs, for Graham was a hard, tough customer. The trees were not ten paces off when a backward look wrung a curse from him. There was a guy on a high-headed clay bank churning the dust in his rear!

Misery taught his bronc what spurs were for, and then put his belt to the business; but the distance between himself and that hell-tearing ranny behind remained just about the same. The man had as good a nag as Jones himself, and was equally bent on proving it.

It was a bad sign, the tenacity with which that hombre clung to the trail; and Jones began squinting around for a place to lay up and gun him. But the land thereabouts wasn't built for an ambush, and plainly

Misery would have to climb higher into the tumbled crags if he hoped to stop the man that way.

He rode through the Pass in a gale of wind, and the black's larruping hoofs made a sound like a drum. But the solitary horseman pounding in his wake never lost so much as a jackrabbit's jump; and Misery cursed in a passion.

Noon came and went, and the chase spurred on with hardly a pause for a breather. Misery slackened once and stuck up his warning, a sign which even the youngest Apache could read. It was dangerous to follow his trail. Just a hunk of Misery's shirt-tail tied to a stick; but if the man on the claybank passed it, he was asking for whatever Jones gave him.

But the gent never paused, and Misery grabbed up his rifle. He twisted round in the saddle and drove two spurts of sand across the claybank's legs. The man in the claybank's saddle never slowed his bronc a fraction.

It was beginning to get on Jones' nerves.

The black took him roaring over the crest of a hogback, and a thicket of squatting alders broke the dun expanse to the left. Jones slammed Hawswell's black straight into it and flung down out of the saddle. He lay down flat on his belly and pushed his new Sharps rifle through the brush and maliciously squinted down his sights. When the fellow crossed them, he fired.

A clean miss! With an oath. Misery forked his saddle and the chase went on again.

The afternoon wore on. Misery was forced to stop more frequently now or risk the loss of his horse. But every time he stopped the man on the claybank likewise stopped; and quick as Jones started he started.

It was enough to make a preacher curse, and Misery was no preacher.

Misery drifted down the valley with his glance twisted over his shoulder. The wind was getting rougher now; it moaned through the brush and bent the trees, and the grit hit hard as hail. Misery prayed for a sandstorm so that he could shake the leech who followed him.

Then suddenly the storm struck down, and the air was filled with fury and the light dimmed out to a mudbrown haze that was thick as a chocolate fog. Misery stopped his bronc in the lee of some junipers and forced the creature to lie down. Then he snuggled up to it and pulled his tarp up over his head to wait till the storm went elsewhere.

It was close to dusk when it finally ceased. Misery got up and thankfully stretched. He shook the sand from his tarp, rolled it up and tied it back of his cantle. Then he got his bronc up and was lifting his boot to the stirrup when a dark blotch of shadow caught his eye through the junipers' branches; and he took one hard look and cursed. For he had stopped on one side of the trees and the claybank's rider had stopped on the other—and the fellow was looking right at him.

"Well," said the man with a *whoosh* of breath, "you're about as sorry a buck as I've ever chased for puttin' a gent to hard bother! Criminy Christmas an' hellity larrup! I—"

"Me, too!" Misery blared with a curse; and fetched out a gun with his thumb on the hammer.

"Hold on!" puffed the man in a lather of hurry. "You got me plumb wrong—*I* ain't after yore hide! There ain't no more harm in Short Beer Ballard than you could squeeze from a bucket of turnips. I'm peaceful as the day is long—pure quill wool an' twenty yards wide—"

"So's my A'nt Hester!" snapped Misery. "You get them paws stretched high as they'll reach or I'll blast yo' from that saddle! Just what did you reckon you was doin', eh? Chasin' me 'round like a wild bull! I've a dang good mind to plant you heah—an' who'll ever be the wiser, eh? Stretch yo' ears, you sabre-toothed whangatang. You shed yo'self of some truth—an' quick, or I'll puncture yo' mortal tintype! Get talkin', fat man!"

The fat stranger rubbed a bristly jaw and hooked a knee over his pommel. He was shaggy and huge as a hived-up grizzly, with hair as red as vermilion paint where it straggled from under his horse thief hat; and his eyes were a cool hard hazel. Fat he was, and reckless and brittle as a frisky March hare, and with a big gun packed on each hip. Under more pleasant circumstances, Misery thought, he might have cottoned to this fellow, for there was a lurking twinkle in his hard stare, and the shape of his mouth was generous. He wasn't the least bit afraid or embarrassed at finding himself under Misery's gun. In fact, he was suddenly grinning.

"Well, damn your eyes!" Misery growled, "what's so funny?"

"I was thinkin' of the pronto way you lit a shuck back there when I tried to hail you."

"Yeah? Well, you better save up a few of them grins till after I get done with you!"

"Jest as you say, pilgrim. But the' ain't no sense in us fussin' this way—us rebels had ort to stick together. Elsewise, dam' Yankees like this Curly Bill will like to be the death of us."

"So it's Curly Bill, is it? An' what do you know of him? Did he hire you take out after me?"

"Curly Bill hire *me!* Well, that is good! He hates me worse'n pizen, Bill does—he wouldn't hire me to bat flies." The fat man chuckled reminiscently. "I'm Short Beer Ballard, mister, what used to be Curly Bill's straw boss when he was kingpin rustler in these parts—"

"Yeah? Well, that's no recommend to *me*. For all I know you're his straw boss now. I don't figure to go by guesswork, Ballard; just heave yo' guns off in the brush theah."

"You don't seem to get it," Ballard said, grinning. "I *used* to be his straw boss. I quit him cold when he took to stickin' up stages—and that kind of graft is out of my line—"

"All who believe that can go stand on their heads," said Misery Jones Fenner, and snorted. "I'm countin' just three—you can dish out the truth or git planted." Then without more words, Misery tilted his gun at the fat man's chest; and Ballard's grin kind of went twisted.

"Hold on now, sport," he wheezed hurriedly. "I'm handin' you Gospel—no kiddin'. I used to be Curly Bill's right hand, but we ain't even speakin' now—he's got a mad on at me. An' he'll sure be havin' one on you when he finds out how you've larruped him. Brother, I take my hat off—Yes, sir! You've sure made a monkey of him; an' when I see what you was up to I says, 'Short Beer, my boy, there's a pilgrim that's bitin' off more'n he can chew. You better pitch in an' go help him'."

"Very obligin' of you," Misery drawled, "but when I want help *I'll* pick it—"

"You talk like a fool!" Ballard snorted. "When you want help you won't git no time to pick it—take it from me. Curly Bill's got this country plumb sewed up. That sandy you run was plain luck, boy; it ain't like to happen again. He'll hunt you plumb from hell to breakfast—"

"Hoo, hoo!" jeered Misery. "He'll shout, too! You can go back an' tell him I found you right plausible, but I ain't takin' on any sidekicks. I'm a lone wolf critter from the Bitter Crick marshes, an' if he knows what's good for him, your Curly Bill friend will steer his steps clear away from me."

"Okey by me."

Ballard shrugged and sighed and picked up his reins. Then he hesitated. He seemed to scan some thought stored away in his head, and with a dour grin he said:

"You'd better watch out for that Broken Bow bunch—special Hawswell an' that young Dude Fenner. They're in with Curly Bill up to their ears, an' they're sure goin' to nail your hide to the fence when they find out what you been up to."

"Now that's a plain unvarnished lie!" snapped Misery, spurred heels jumping his horse against Ballard's bronc. "Curly Bill hired me to go out there an' put them Fenners—"

"Yeah—he tried that gag on me once, too. He's crooked as a snake's hindquarters. But that don't prove Dude Fenner ain't in with him. Why I could tell you—"

"Don't waste yo' breath! I know Dude Fenner a sight better than you—"

"All right, mister; it's no grief of mine." Ballard shook his reins and jogged his bronc off toward Galeyville.

But he had got hardly any way at all when Misery Jones Fenner with a curse sent Hawswell's horse ploughing after him. Just as Jones came up with Ballard a third horseman showed over the crest of a hogback and pulled his horse up beside them. It was Petro Petralgo, the long-geared Mex with the broken nose that Misery had met several nights before on the trail to the Fenner ranch. He was a slick talking customer who got straight-away down to brass tacks.

It was Ballard Petralgo spoke to, and his words were couched in a sneer.

"You are ridin' in the mighty bad company, Senor Short Beer," he observed. "I thought Curly Beel ron you out of thees contry. . . ."

"Well now, I can't think what ever give you that notion," Ballard drawled, rolling up a smoke. "I been over in Texas visitin' my wife's kinsfolk."

"I didn't know you' had a wife."

"Well, I ain't. But I woulda had if my ol' man hadn't put a codicil in his will that cuts me off from all his money if I marry beneath my station. O' course, my station in this here vale of tears is open to considerable argument, but my lawyer tells me a Blackfoot squaw could legally be so considered."

Petralgo eyed him with a fishy stare; then abruptly with a scowl he sneered:

"Some more of your goddam jokes, I guess. You better clear out of here pronto. Curly Beel has swear for to get your hair—"

"Shucks," Ballard said, and chuckled. "How's the stage-robbin' business these days? Got your fortune salted away yet? I'm su'prised you're still hangin' 'round with Bill; I kinda figured after his run-in with the Earps—Oh, well; that's life, I reckon. You an' Bill made enough to retire on yet?"

"Hah! You make the joke—no?"

Petralgo's scowl showed blacker and more vicious, but he was careful to keep his hands in sight, though his back was stiff with resentment.

"Let me tell you something, hombre—" He seemed to champ the words through his teeth as, leaning forward, he tapped Ballard's chest. "Eef you know w'at's good for the health, by gar, you weel cut the wide circle 'round Curly Beel's town—"

"Oh-ho!" Ballard grinned. "So Bill's gone into real estate now! What's he gettin' for lots these days? If it ain't too much I might buy me a couple. I reckon two'd be enough to bury him on; an' he's sure goin' to need some buryin' if he messes 'round with me any more! You jest run along in an' tell him so, will you? I wouldn't want it said around that I'd taken any advantage of him."

Petralgo's flushed cheeks paled with fury; and Misery's left hand dropped to his pistol. But Short Beer Ballard just tipped back his head and gave vent to a hearty guffaw. He laughed till the tears rolled out of his eyes; but he sobered quickly as Petralgo rode out of sight, and he told Jones Fenner grimly:

"You wanta keep your eyes skinned out for that hombre; he's slipperier than calf slobbers and would sell his own gran'mother for a half a centavo. He's Curly Bill's right hand these days—got the job I used to hold down once, and he's up to his ears in every piece of skulduggery that goes on in these localities. He's a loco-weed smoker an' mean as they come, an' if ever he gets a mad on at you you might's well go out an' shoot yourself—"

"I notice you're still takin' nourishment."

"Hmm . . . . Well, I'll tell you. I got the Injun sign on him; but he's killed twelve guys by my personal count. You want to watch out for him. When Bill finds how you've bamboozled him he'll set Petro on your trail sure."

"Are you tryin' to advise me to cut my stick?"

"Nope—I make it a point never to advise nobody. I advised Stonewall Jackson— Oh yes, I used to be his chiefest aide; General Lee always blamed Stonewall's death on me, but I hadn't no part in it really! Hold on there—where you off to?"

"I got all your braggin' I can stand for one day. If I was a rancher," Misery said uncharitably, "I'd hire you to keep my windmills goin'. As it is, kindly get yo'self out of my way—an' be dang sure you don,'t tag after me."

Short Beer Ballard rubbed his extra chins.

"I guess you're going back out to Doc Crawford's place—"

"You know too much about everyone's business, friend."

"I know too much about everyone's business," Ballard assured him without rancour. "That comes down from my Paw, I guess. He used to be a newspaper man. He run the *Washin'ton Star* years ago till he bought out the *Burlington Free Press*—but them dang Vermonters was too much for him; though some lays it on to corn likker. Cousin Effie says his takin' off was entirely unpremeditated. She tells how he grabbed the wrong bottle one night in the dark. . . . Tck, tck, tck!" the fat man clucked dolorously. "But that's the way it goes in this life—there jest plain ain't no justice. Remember that, boy—no matter what the textbooks say. You take it from Short Beer Ballard, son— "

"You go to hell!" said Misery, and wheeled his horse to get himself out of the racket. His mind fair reeled under the staggering burden of Short Beer's words, and he spurred his horse to a gallop. Small wonder, he thought, Curly Bill had ordered the man from the country! Why, he'd talk a deaf man's arm off!

But one thing Ballard had said stuck in Misery's memory. The fat man had called old Crawford "Doc"—and the truth about that was worth finding out. But when he came in sight of the Crawford place, all thought of the old man's being a sawbones was completely crowded from his mind.

The night was black as the inside of a cat, with no moon showing and the star haze half concealed behind cloud; but it was not too dark for Misery Jones to see the fine sad-dled bronc that was hitched to the post by the door. He had a dark suspicion then which got prompt confirmation when he stepped inside. It was visitor's night at the claimshack; and Dude Fenner had the best chair!

Chapter 7

Dude was all dressed up like a dang potato bug. There was a tall beaver hat on the floor by his chair; his curls were combed in the height of fashion and they gleamed with a barber's lotions. Misery blushed to think that such a dude was his brother. Fenner's weak chin was swathed in a high flaring collar above a bow stock, his waistcoat was bright as a butterfly's wings, and the ample pale blue coat he wore over it had a wide rolled collar and tails behind. His tight-fitting pants—of brilliant stripe pattern— were strapped under varnished boots. And Misery's jaundiced stare picked out a pair of gloves and a polished cane on the floor beside the Dude's hat.

"Why, Misery!" Taisy cried gladly, and came hurrying forward to take Misery's cream-coloured Stetson. "We thought you had gone—cleared out of the country. Mr. Fenner was telling us you had. . . ."

"Yeah!" Misery scowled, and kept hold of his hat. "Well, yo'll find Mister Fenner's mistaken—I ain't cleared out by a long shot!"

Morgan Crawford said hurriedly:

"And glad we are to hear it, my boy. We were taken aback to think you had gone without even saying good-bye." Then he smiled. "You're looking mighty prosperous. Have you made a good connection?"

"I don't know about that." Misery scowled at his brother. "To tell you the truth, I been speculatin'. You might say I've taken a flyer in real estate—"

"Why, that's wonderful," said Crawford warmly. "Any investment in this Arizona land is bound to be sound and profitable. Going to build up with the country, are you?"

Taisy gave him a breath-taking smile, but Dude Fenner frostily ignored him. He sat twiddling the massive gold chain that was conspicuously draped across the front of him, and Misery decided to give him a jolt. He said:

"I've just made a deal on the Fenner ranch—I've sold the whole works to Bill Graham."

He could hardly have produced more consternation had he shot both the Dude's ears off.

Young Fenner leapt out of his chair as if a scorpion had crawled up his pants leg.

"You've *what?*"

"I guess you heard me," Jones grinned. "I've just sold your spread to Bill Graham—"

"Why, you dastardly blackguard!" Dude Fenner snarled, and slammed a hand under his waistcoat.

"Let him go," Misery said to Crawford, who had made haste to grab the Dude's elbow. "Go on—let the guinea-pig squeal if he wants to. Let him pull his gun; I'll knock him so far it'll take a bloodhound a week to catch up to him!"

The Dude's handsome face was purple with wrath, but Morgan Crawford hung on to him grimly, and Taisy, shocked, cried out reproachfully:

"But, Misery! You had no right to sell Broken Bow Ranch."

Misery's hard grin crossed his tight lips, and he nodded.

"What I told Graham. But he claimed it was legal enough for *him.* If he's suited, I don't reckon I got any kick—"

"You dirty crook!" Dude Fenner snarled. "I'll put you back of bars for this!"

"Oh-ho! So the pot calls the kettle black!

70

Goin' to put me back of bars, are you? Hoo, hoo! You-an' who else?" Misery jeered. "You let me know the day, sonny, an' I'll clean up sellin' tickets!"

Morgan Crawford frowned. "I'm surprised at you, son."

And Taisy, flushed and stormy-eyed, declared indignantly:

"But you had no right to do such a thing! You ought to be ashamed—"

"Oh! Ashamed, is it?" Misery scowled. "So you're all gangin' up on me, are you? All takin' up for this short sport that would turn his own relatives away from the door—for this whoppy-jawed chipmunk that would sell his own brother for a handful of silver!" He pulled his back up straight as a ramrod and glared at them all contemptuously. "Well, go ahead! I guess I know when my company ain't wanted!"

He wheeled on his heel and slammed into the night, wrathfully banging the door behind him.

He climbed on the horse he had taken from Hawswell and rode for three hours without stopping. By that time some of the rage had cooled out of him and he was able to view recent events with a calmer perception. Perhaps the sandy he had run on Curly Bill Graham *hadn't* been strictly honest as judged by drawing-room standards—but this was no case for such judgment. He had just given Graham back some of his own; and he would do it again if chance offered. Misery was a staunch believer in Old Testament values, and "an eye for an eye" was his motto. None of this cheek-turning stuff for him—as Dude Fenner should learn to his cost!

It riled him every time he thought about Dude. He was just a young upstart, a high-stomached Johnny-Come-Lately who was headed for hell by the shortest path; a brand for the burning and a plain downright challenge to all who bore the Fenner name. A challenge Misery sure aimed to take up.

He would show the dang young whipper-snapper! It sure was hard lines to see this city slicker stuff cropping out in a man's own brother. Seemed like the Dude was turning out to be a throwback to old Rip Fenner, his great-great-uncle, who was the skeleton in the Fenners' family closet and who had been caught red-handed at piracy and hanged from a man-a'-war's yardarm. But the Dude was not going to be hanged—not if Misery had any say in it! He would mend his ways and mend them pronto or—well, there would sure be some mighty dire consequences.

That there might be truth in Ballard's story Misery would not consider for a second. The idea of any Fenner hobnobbing around with an outlaw like that sidewinding Curly Bill put too much strain on Misery's imagination. He would not countenance such a notion. That the Fenner foreman, Hawswell, might be mixed up with Graham seemed to Misery very likely—but never a Fenner—*never!* No man bearing that proud name could ever stoop so low!

Even in his righteous anger at the unpleasant qualities he had found in Dude—the hateful traits and despicable meanness—he could not conceive any brother of his having fallen so low as to be knowingly hooked up with an outlaw. So the Short Beer gent was just plain wrong—mistaken, or else maliciously spreading a false rumour.

Misery sighed when he thought of his father. Old Joe had aged a great deal in three years; and small wonder, with the way the Dude was acting up. It was enough to make a plaster wrinkle.

Misery had only sympathy for old Joe. His sight was failing, Crawford had said; that was why he had not recognized Misery.

Maybe his hearing was afflicted, too. When a man started going, he fell apart fast. Poor Pa! He'd been such a ripping good sport in the old days. Fenner Hall had been famed for its hospitality from El Paso del Norte clear to Dallas. And Old Joe had been famed, too—famed for his rare understanding, for the gift of his way with "his boys".

There was moisture in Jones Fenner's stare as he thought of old Joe and the past. The last three years had gone hard with him, and the war had thrown him on evil days— but Misery would make it up to him. By grab, yes—and to spare! That was one thing about the Fenners—they stuck through thick and thin. If you picked on one Fenner you picked on them all—as that dang Curly Bill should discover!

Misery thought some while of the Crawfords, too—particularly of Taisy Crawford. Golly! what a girl she was! Loyal as a—a—a cocker spaniel, and as full of fight as a bulldog! A rueful grin crossed his face as he recalled how she had pitched into him in indignant defence of the Dude. And he recalled the stormy look in her eyes as she'd given him that lecture on "rights." He scowled when he thought of that part. What could a sheltered girl like her know about rights in a country like this? Nothing; of course! How could she?

An impatient snort was his answer to that question. But, just the same, she was a mighty fine girl; a girl in a million, sure enough, and she'd make some gent a fine wife. Not *him*, of course—Misery Jones was not the marrying kind; no sir, not by a jugfull None of your frills and flounces for him! But she was too danged good for the likes of the Dude; and he'd tell him so next time he saw him.

The next time he looked up from his musing Dawn was putting its rose-pink blush all across the eastern skyline, and the sight of a shack turned his thoughts toward grub, and the appetizing aromas being wafted along with the smoke curling from the place's chimney made Misery realize he was ravenous.

He wondered what the chances were for a taste of the grub being cooked over there; he decided to stop and find out. It was just a tumble-down line-rider's shack that no line-rider would dare keep in such shape. The occupants were pretty sure to be nesters—though the horse Misery saw in the shaky corral was a black and a pretty danged good one.

Still, Misery reflected, occasionally you did come across a sodbuster who had a good eye for a horse. Everything about yon shack showed neglect, and the garden was knee-high with weeds. They could probably use the money all right, and Misery could do with a meal.

So he reined Hawswell's bronc over and knocked on the door; and when it was opened he said, "Mornin', folks—howdy." And then he stopped short with a whistle. For the girl who stood there holding the door was no sodbuster's dame by a jugful. Pretty as a speckled pup under a new red wagon! Danged near as pretty as Taisy, he thought; but her face was more piquant, more worldly with knowledge, and the look of her eye was more knowing.

She laughed at his whistle, and asked:

"Won't you come in? Grub's on the table and we're ready to sit. . . ."

"Well, now, thank you, ma'am, an' kindly," Jones grinned. "If it won't put you out, I'll just *do* that. That bacon smells uncommon temptin'—"

"It's only fried side-meat," she said, "but you're welcome. Stranger 'round here, aren't you?" she asked as Misery, inside, closed the door.

"Excuse *me!* The name is Misery Jones, ma'am. I ain't been 'round more'n a week or so, but I sure am figurin' on stayin'."

"Mother—this is Misery Jones. Mister Jones, my mother—Mrs. Flystrom."

The old lady jerked a nod at him and brushed a grey strand from her faded eyes. A frail, anaemic body she was, and all muffled up in a wheel chair.

"Set down," she said gruffly; "set down, young man. Julie, lay another plate and hustle before my tea gets cold."

Jones saw a sullen flush cross the girl's cheeks as she clacked her high heels toward the cupboard, a whoppy-jawed cabinet hung from the rafters and curtained with faded calico. But when she came back with a steel knife and fork, a tin plate and a hot cup of coffee, she flashed him a smile over the old lady's head; and somehow Jones felt uncomfortable.

But he pulled up a stool and sat down; then got up and, "Yo' pardon, ma'am," he apologized, and wheeled Mrs. Flystrom up to the table. But a grunt was all he got for it.

The girl came up with a pan from the stove and served each plate a good portion. Then she brought some biscuits out of the stove, and a cracked cup that was half full of sugar, and three tin spoons from a drawer.

"We used to have milk, but someone's run off our cow, so you'll have to take your coffee black—"

"That's just the way I crave it, ma'am," Jones said, and gallantly held a chair for her.

"Set down," the old woman croaked, and regarded Misery uncharitably. "My girl's not used to such grand manners, and I don't mean she shall get to be. We're common folks here, and we know our place. Haul your chair up, Julie, and quit actin' like quality. You'll get no place apin' your betters."

Jones stared, astonished at the old lady's sharpness. He was too polite to look at the girl, but he made a try at smoothing things over. He said:

"I reckon we all do that sometimes. To err is only human—"

"Yes; and virtue is its own reward," answered Mrs. Flystrom tartly; and forthwith fell to eating.

Jones ate too, but he had felt a lot more comfortable when eating at the Crawfords. He wished he had kept his temper last night so that he might be eating there now. But he did his best to make conversation—though his talk was mostly monologue—the old lady contributing nothing herself, and having a hard look ready every time Julie opened her mouth.

Misery thought it a danged queer outfit. He said presently:

"The Crawfords tell me you're home-steading here—"

"So you know them, do you?" the old woman glared. "What else did they tell you about us?"

"Why—er, that's all, I reckon. They jest mentioned you were homesteading a piece of the Fenner range—"

The old lady sniffed, and blew at her coffee gustily.

"The Fenners," she said acidly, "have no more title to this land than the King of Spain has to Portugal. This is Gover'ment ground an' open to entry, an' my daughter's properly filed on it. *And,*" she added with a hard, chill glare, "I'll thank you to remember it!"

Jones gulped down his side-meat and wished he'd had the wit to keep on riding when he'd seen this shack.

Julie said with a flustered smile:

"Now, Mother—" And to Misery: "We came out here for Mother's health. The doctors said this climate—"

"Hush, Julie! Mister Jones ain't interested

in the troubles of any nesters. You ought to see by his clothes he's a cowman—which is only once removed from being cousin to the devil. They're all alike. So God-fearin' smooth butter wouldn't melt in their mouths, but underneath they got no more use for nesters than they'd have for soap or church service! You'd ought to know—"

It was on the tip of Jones' tongue to tell the old girl a thing or two; but a look flicked at Julie changed his mind, and he gulped down his coffee and picked up his hat. Shoving his chair back, he said, "I'm plumb obliged for the meal, folks; it sure slid down mighty easy." He hesitated a second and then reached for his wallet; but the old lady guessed his intention. Her eyes took on a brighter glint.

"We feed the Philistines free," she said: and Misery bit down a curse. But for the sake of the girl he told her:

"That's mighty friendly of you, ma'am. I'm on my way to town," he added, "an' if there's any thing I could fetch—"

"We're accepting no favours from cowmen."

There was no taint of friendship in the old woman's tone; like her eye, it was cold as a well chain.

Misery muttered under his breath and commenced feeling around for the door. The pink-cheeked Julie started forward, but the old lady's shrill voice blared like a trumpet:

"Julie! He can find the door without your help! Get back to that chair an' set down!"

Jones clapped his hat down hard on his head and made haste to get on his pony.

"Fella 'd think," he muttered, roan-cheeked, "I was took with the smallpox or somethin'!"

Chapter 8

It was certainly a queer outfit he had met at the line-rider's cabin; but no more queer, Misery thought with a scowl, than that he should be meeting Ballard again almost before he got out of earshot of the clack of the old woman's tongue. Short Beer stepped from a tangle of catclaw with his bronc's reins over his arm and a whimsical grin on his rotund face. His left lid dropped in a sly kind of wink as, with a chuckle, he said:

"What'd you wanta go an' pick on that helpless old lady for? I'm surprised at you, boy; I done took you for a gentleman."

"This is the damnedest country I ever been in," Misery growled.

"Yes sir," Ballard assured him. "Right here is that land you heard about where the hoot-owls bed with the chickens—an' speakin' of beds, I'd advise you to keep plumb away from them Flystroms, partic'lar that buxom filly. The ol' woman done caught her out in the barn with Dude Fenner las' month; an' it's turned 'er plumb sour on all cowmen."

Misery went stiff as a board in his saddle. His look was a mixture of incredulity and wrath.

"*What's that?* You say Dude Fenner—"

"Yep—that Dude is the one. I'd take my oath on a stack o' Bibles high as that there cottonwood. It chances I was passin' by at the time an' I saw the Dude hightailin' it. The ol' woman's tongue was cuttin' real capers, an' the Dude wasn't losin' any time clearin' out. An' he had a look on his mug that was like a tenderfoot trapper skinnin' a skunk. I tell you, if that ol' girl had had a rifle, the Dude's career woulda been cut plumb short!"

A tide of colour surged above Misery's collar and rushed clean into the roots of his hair. Then his cheeks got white and his eyes got like blue Yukon ice with a moon on it.

"Now hold on, son—" cried Short Beer hastily. "Don't go takin' that mad out on *me*. How was I to know you was sweet on Julie? I didn't even s'pose you knowed her—I was just tryin' to pass you a friendly tip—"

He backed off in alarm as Misery jumped from the saddle. But Jones was too full of his own thoughts even to notice Ballard's antics. His left hand caught the fat Short Beer's shoulder and shook him as if he were a sack of oats.

"By grab, you better have proof—"

"Great guns!" Ballard gasped through chattering teeth. "I never said they *did* nothin', durn it! Far's I know the girl's—"

"You said Dude Fenner—"

"Was in the barn with her an' the ol' woman caught 'em—an' she sure as hell did! Cripes! Unloose my shoulder! Gawd!" he gasped as Misery stepped back. "I feel plumb like a bull had gored me! You dunno what a grip—Here! Hold on! Where you goin'?"

"I'm goin' to see Dude Fenner!"

"Oh, mercy me!" cried Short Beer, scared-like. "You goin' in that orful tone o' voice? Lord save us all! Wait"—he wheezed, fishing around for his stirrup, "I'm—"

But Misery wasn't waiting for anything. He was into his saddle and off in a cloud of dust. And still looking scared, Ballard ploughed in his wake.

It was nine, by the sun, when they topped a crest and saw the Broken Bow buildings. The yard was deserted, which would seem to indicate that the Fenner riders were off on the range at their appointed tasks. But old Joe Fenner was in the porch-rocked with his glance far off toward the blue horizon and his gnarled old hands folded over his cane.

Misery stopped by the horse-pen.

"Wait here," he said, and tossed Ballard his reins.

Then he stepped like a cat to the Fenner porch, with a look on his cheeks like the wrath of God.

"Suh—I'm lookin' fo Dude Fenner!"

Slowly the old man's head came around. He eyed Jones Fenner with casual inquiry. Then a dour light showed in his faded glance and he said:

"Haven't I seen you some place—?"

"I shouldn't wonder. Where is he?"

"Where's who?"

"That insolent cub of a no-good John Fenner-"

"You'll have to speak louder, son. I'm a mite hard of hearin'."

"I'm huntin' Dude Fenner—"

"You say you're lookin' for good weather? Humph! Mostly always good in Arizony, ain't it?"

Jones glared. It almost seemed as if the old man were funning him; then he remembered that this was his father, and he curbed his impatience—got a hold on his temper. This was old Joe Fenner, who was always polite and would no more think of ridiculing a stranger than he'd think of heaving lead at his livestock. The old man just didn't hear well, that was all. Jones tried again, and this time he shouted.

"I'm huntin' your son! John Fenner—the Dude!"

"Oh, you're lookin' for John. Well, he's not here, my boy."

Old Joe shook his head. Then he ran a trembling hand through his hair. "Would there be anything I could take care of for ye? The Dude's gone to town—something to do with the ranch work. Like enough he'll be back here come supper. Will ye wait?"

Jones Fenner scowled. Then he, too, shook his head.

"No—I'll drop by again." Then, abruptly, he said, "Don't you recognize me, Paw?"

The old man stared, then muttered querulously:

"You'll have to speak louder, boy." He tapped an ear several times with his finger while he peered nearsightedly in the direction of Misery. "I don't hear so good. What was it ye was asking?"

But Misery sighed and turned back towards his horse. It was hard, bitter hard; but there was no way around it, looked like. He guessed the old man would never know him. What use to shout? Old Joe had the Government's paper, and even if Misery could make himself understood, the old man wouldn't believe him. And, besides, there was Ballard over there with the horses, with his ears hung out like a hound dog's tongue. He'd be passing any gossip he gathered right on, and Jones had no wish to have his business discussed all over these mountains.

"Not home, eh?" said Ballard, relieved-like.

Misery grunted and climbed into his saddle. He picked up his reins, and waved good-bye to Old Joe. Short Beer said:

"Where are we off to now?"

"*I*'m off to town," Misery said. "Where you go ain't worryin' me."

Ballard sniffed.

"Reckon I'll go to town, too," he said. "I could do with a snort of red-eye. I ain't been so dry since the time Stonewall Jackson—"

"For the love of Mike, turn it off a while—give it a rest. Don't you ever get fed up with the sound of that voice?"

"Which voice?" Ballard said, peering around.

Jones kicked spurs to his bronc, and nothing more was said for some miles. Misery appeared to be deep in thought.

"Schemin' out somethin', I'll bet," Ballard grunted to himself. Then he asked, "How come you was in such a lather gettin' away from the Crawfords' las' night?"

Misery whirled on him wrathfully.

"Is Curly Bill hirin' you to foller me?"

"Is—*huh!* I should say not! He wouldn't hire me to bat flies off his burro! Him an' me ain't speakin' these days—"

"An' how was that accomplished? I'd pay good money to get the recipe!"

But Short Beer Ballard refused to be insulted. He just heaved up a chuckle from out of his depths and waggled his head good-naturedly.

"Be *worth* good money, mister. But I'll tell you how it is with me; when I cotton to a fella I *cotton* to him—"

"I don't need no bodyguard."

"You never can tell. This is danged unsettled country," Ballard said portentously. "A man never knows from the cradle to the grave—"

"All right. Just leave it that way. Mebbe I'd rather find out for myself."

"But a man shouldn't leave things to chance like that. The wise man looks ahead in this world.

"Just what in hell are you gettin' at?"

"Why, Curly Bill, of course! I always say—"

"You certainly do!" Misery growled, and gave his bronc the spurs again in an effort to leave Short Beer behind. But the self-confessed ex-member of Curly Bill's wild bunch was well mounted, and he didn't take Misery's dust for long.

When he appeared alongside, Short Beer grumbled with a disconsolate shake of the head:

"It all comes of me partin' with that shoe, I reckon. . . ."

"*Now* what you talkin' about?"

"Why, that danged lucky horseshoe that's

88

been in our fambly since the days o' William the Conqueror—Didn't I ever tell you 'bout that shoe? Well, step on my cinches! It all come of my generosity. When I left home t' join up, my ol' man reached up over the door an' he hauled down this lucky shoe for me. 'Take it, son,' he says, 'an' allus keep 'er by you. That was worn by General Ney's great charger in the famous battle at Moskwa. Somebody stole it after-wards, an' Ney never had no more luck. So let his fate be a warnin' to yuh an' don't never part with it ever'."

Short Beer fetched a doleful sigh, and his three chins shivered drearily.

"My ol' man shore knowed what he was talkin' about. It was a ill-fated day when I done tacked that shoe on Stonewall's hawss—yes, sir, one o' the darkest days o' my life. But the General was a danged fine sport an' lucky as a bucket of rabbit's hooves so long as he had that shoe. Not that he knowed he had it—I was a sight too modest them days to tell what I had done fer him. But one night, right in the thick of the battle, I heard the ol' boy give a gasp, an' down he went out of his saddle, just like a bagful o' birdshot. I couldn't figure how the hell he'd got hit till next mornin'. I took that hawss o' his 'round to the Chancellorsville blacksmith first thing befo' breakfast, an' do you know what? That daggone bronc had throwed away our fambly's lucky shoe!"

Misery gave him a sideways look and snorted.

"You better be savin' up some of that bull to dish out to Graham when we get to town. He's apt to be on the warpath."

"You sure told it that time, fella. Curly Bill's goin' to be in a real roaring mood an' no mistake. I wouldn't be in your boots fer a barrel of monkeys! He'll sure give you a new hair-comb—"

"Oh, he will, eh?" grunted Misery, turning suddenly grim again, and Short Beer made haste to change the subject.

"Have you ever done any prospectin', Jones? Reckon you'd know the real thing from pyrites? Reason I ask is I've found a hole over by Hitchens' Bottoms. There's some stuff over there—"

But Misery wasn't listening. He was thinking of Dude, his brother John Fenner, and his look was patterned on agate.

No more was said till they were loping along the Turkey Creek bottoms; then Short Beer said kind of tentatively:

"Mebbe you better rest your hawws down here till I ride up an' scout what's doin'."

But Misery just snorted.

"You needn't be frettin' about Curly Bill. 'Live an' let live' is my motto. Long as—"

"Yeah," Ballard said; "but it might be that Bill wouldn't know that."

"That'll be Mister Graham's tough luck then," Jones said; but he rode with both eyes peeled carefully. Because, despite his brave talk, he was well aware Bill would be hog-wild to get even.

They pulled up in front of Shotwell's store, and Jones went rampaging right in as if he were no more scared of Bill Graham's being around than a chipmunk would be of a dobson.

Shotwell's face lost two shades of colour when he looked up and recognized Misery.

"My gosh! You back here again! I figgered we'd seen the last o' you—"

"Humph!" Jones said. "You seen anything of Dude Fenner?"

"You'd better keep away from the Dude," Shotwell said. But a long-geared gent leaning on the counter told him:

"You'll find the Dude over in Babcock's bar. He's hoisting a couple with Curly Bill Graham."

Misery turned right round, heading streetwards again; and the long-geared gent unravelled himself from the counter and, with a broad wink at Shotwell sauntered leisurely after him, hands hooked by their thumbs to his gun-belt.

At the hitch rack Ballard stopped Jones.

"That guy back there," he said with a grunt, "is Al George—a friend o' Bill's. Keep your eye skinned. George's a bad actor. He shot a butcher yesterday just for wavin' a paper in front of George's hawss."

"Yeah—he's enough to cramp rats," Misery snarled; and without even looking in George's direction he forked his bronc over to Babcock's.

There were a couple of men lounging alongside the door, and Ballard said quickly:

"Tough hombres, boy. That big squirt is Jerry Barton; he notches his gun an' don't never count the same man twice—an' there ain't a danged notch fer a Mexican. That other fella is Jaw Bone Clark—he runs a dance hall. Step careful, boy, 'cause he's in a bad mood. Judge Burnett run sho't in a poker game last night an' fined him for bein' drunk; an' when the Judge's chips got low again, he arrested Jaw Bone for disturbin' the peace, an' nicked him fifty bucks more."

Misery never even glanced at them. He

pushed right through Babcock's batwings and strode determined right up to the bar.

"I'm lookin' for a pole cat named Fenner—Dude Fenner," he said loudly; and all the talk quit on the instant.

Ballard groaned, and backed off towards the end of the bar as unostentatiously as possible. Misery followed the look of men's eyes and saw Dude Fenner scowling from a chair beside Curly Bill at a table far down the room.

Curly Bill wasn't scowling; a quick, glad light glinted from his dark eyes, and the shine of his teeth came through his lips as Misery swung down the room towards them.

If Misery was scared you wouldn't have guessed it; and Curly Bill's face went thoughtful. There were not many men in Cherrycows who would have faced him this way after what Misery had done; and that fact had its weight with Bill pronto. He had been all cocked for action; but he let the tough look slide from his face as Misery stopped by the table.

"There he is!" Dude Fenner cried, half starting up, with his face black as thunder, and his shaking fist pointed square at Misery.

"You're golrammed tootin'!" Misery

flung right back. "I want you, young fella—jest step outside. There's a matter that's needin' adjustin—"

"Just a minute!" Curly Bill leaned forward and rapped on the table with his big, blunt fingers. "You hit the nail right smack on the head! There's a lot of things needin' adjustin'—just pull up a chair and sit down."

Misery looked at him coldly.

"I don't believe I know you," he said; and Curly Bill very nearly choked.

With a lofty look down his nose at him, Misery said to Dude Fenner:

"Come along, John; we're keepin' the lady waitin'."

The Dude didn't appear to know up from down; and Curly Bill, clawing out of his chair, with a strangled oath reached for Misery.

But Jones backed off and Graham's clutch fell short; and suddenly Jones had a gun out.

"Be careful, hombre. I'm some particular who I let hug me, and there ain't no worms on the list."

He heard the chorus of gasps that riffled the barroom's smoke; and Curly Bill Graham heard them likewise. His eyes went wicked and his big fists bunched; but Misery didn't even look at him.

"Come along," he said again to the Dude. "It ain't right to keep a bride waitin'.'"

"A bride!" Fenner gasped. "What in hell's name are you talking about?"

"About *you,* an' yo' approachin' nuptials. Don't claim you've forgotten! An' the dear girl weepin' her eyes out account of you not showin' up like you promised! For shame, Mister Fenner—for shame!"

The Dude stood there like a fish out of water; and some of the crowd started snickering till Misery's stern eye brushed across them. Then the batwings swung open, and Barton came in with a gun in each fist, and Jaw Bone glared over his shoulder.

"What's that bird got a gun on you for? You want I should pop 'im, Bill?" Barton growled.

"Pop ahead," Misery said without turning. "Yo' first pop will pull Graham's curtain."

Then Ballard—from the end of the bar—said:

"Never mind them, boy. The next peep outa them civet cats will get 'em stretched out on a shutter."

"All right, Fenner. Tramp on outside—an' while I think of it," Misery told Curly Bill, "you better step along with him. Start workin' yo' pedals, both of you."

The Dude looked at Graham but got little help, for Curly Bill had his own hands full.

"This farce," he rasped, "has gone far enough!"

But Jones' pistol never wavered from its focus on Curly Bill's vest; and with a sudden, inarticulate snarl, he clanked his spurs toward the batwings. Dude Fenner followed reluctantly.

The Dude glared around when he got outside; then he reared back on his bootheels.

"I don't see no damn woman!" he snarled.

Yet if there was in him any gratefulness towards Misery for having dragged him out of that iniquitous den, a man would have been hard put to guess it.

He planted his varnished boots fit to sprout them.

"Not another damn step!" he spat out bitterly. "Not another blasted step will I go till I've been told what the devil you're up to!"

He drew himself up to the fullest height and clamped his arms folded as if he would pass himself off for Lucifer; and well he might, Misery grimly thought, if he'd a plume for his hat and a dagger!

Jones eyed the Dude contemptuously.

"You're enough to cramp rats! For a couple of shucks I would throw you over an' let you go straight wheah yo' headed! Trouble is, bad as you are, you're still a Fenner; an' I suppose it's worth some kind of effort to keep the name outa the mud. But I'm servin' warnin' right here an' now! You quit chummin' 'round with snakes like this Graham or I'll sure lug you off to a horspital!"

That talk put the Dude in a pretty poor light, but he scowled down his nose disdainfully.

"Ballard!"

Short Beer came puffing.

"You go hunt me up this Judge Burnett," Misery said, "an' don't waste time pickin' posies."

"He lives jest around that corner there—"

"Get him!" Misery paused to focus his gun more ominously toward Graham's belly. "Go fetch im, Ballard, and see that he's got a horse he can ride. You tell him this is urgent—that a man's life may be hangin' on his speed. An' it ain't no lie," he added; for Bill Graham's look was a promise.

But Jones kept his drop on the owl-hooter, and Graham had to glare in baulked fury.

"There's goin' to be a hereafter for *you!*" gritted Graham, being fully cognizant of the large crowd taking this in from the safety of adjacent coverts. "I'm goin' to make you wish you never was born!"

But Misery grinned at him sneeringly.

"If I was half as puny as you," he jeered, "I'd not be doin' s'much braggin'. Now hush up 'fore this crowd thinks you're scared of me."

Curly Bill's eyes stuck out like a mackerel's.

Ballard came back with the Justice in tow, and the old man was bleary-eyed and cranky.

"I ort to fine you," he growled, "fer disturbin' the peace!"

Misery pulled out his wallet like lightning.

"The fine's accepted. How much, Judge?"

Burnett lowered his shotgun.

"Um—er—*forty dollars*" he said quietly; and Misery gave him eighty.

"Well" the Judge said, mollified. "I can see you're going to be an asset to this community." Then he glared at the glowering Curly Bill, and asked, "What's that damn scamp up to *this* time?"

"He's goin' to aide an' abet a weddin', Judge. Here's the bridegroom," Misery said, pointing to Fenner. "Don't you reckon Bill will do for best man?"

The Judge eyed Dude uncharitably.

"I don't know who'd care to marry this feller, but if there's any girl willin' I guess she won't find too much fault with Bill Graham. You want to watch him, though. He's slippery as slobbers, an' if he bats a eye I'd advise you to salivate him pronto. If you don't, I'll shore do it myself!"

It was a sad, sad day for Curly Bill's pride when he led that procession out of town on the trail that led through the San Simon Pass, with the gaping-mouthed stares of the whole population following.

Chapter 9

Misery Jones had hardly left the Crawfords' cabin striding stormily into the windswept night, before Taisy, pleading a sick headache, excused herself to the Dude and her father and retired, very pale, to her room. She felt really sick, and she buried her face in her pillow and sobbed; for she knew now that Misery was no real knight like the ones in the books. He was just what Dude Fenner had called him—a tough, unscrupulous drifter; and Taisy cried as if her heart would break.

But next morning she felt better. The day

had dawned auspiciously, and she had put on her blue denim overalls and gone for a ride on her pony. To her father she said she had need of exercise; but she really rode off so as to he alone where she could give her mind to her problems without danger of interruption.

And that thinking did her a world of good; and the exercise helped her too, like as not, for it worked off some of her energy and let her mind face her troubles squarely. In the bright golden light of the fresh new morn her life seemed not so filled with snarls as last night she had imagined it.

To he sure, Misery Jones was far from the knight her youthful fancy had imagined him. Yet for all his so-human weaknesses, he did have one shining virtue—that utter disregard of fear. He was no more scared of Bill Graham, seemed like, than she would be of her shadow. Imagine any man daring to trick Curly Bill as Misery had done! It was stupendous, really; and she secretly shivered for Misery to think he could act with such brashness.

And after all, what he had done was not so terribly bad, she supposed, when measured in the light of this country's rough standards. All things in this land were wild and untamed, and it took a bold spirit to face them. Curly Bill had tried to trick Misery into putting the Fenners off their ranch; Misery had but dealt him back some of his own. But she could imagine what her friends back in the Eastern cities would have said!

She determined not to dwell on that, and urged her pony to a faster lope to purge the thought from her mind. And, shortly after, a soft smile curved her lips, for, despite his faults and the flaws in his armour, Misery had won her heart.

He might be a drifter, as Dude Fenner claimed; a rough and unpolished barbarian. And quite often his language stood in need of pruning. But for all that he was a fine figure of a man, and his grin was exciting—it made your heart pound—and he could be real gallant when he wasn't angry. It was only when people crossed him that he went off into one of his tantrums.

It was long after noon when she returned to the house; and it took her some time to rub down her horse and hang its gear up in the harness shed. Her father had gone off somewhere; so she busied herself tidying up the house. Afterwards she went out in the kitchen and brewed some tea and fixed up a couple of sandwiches.

She was just seated comfortably and munching the first when, through the window, she spied a great dust coming down the trail; and she hurried outside to see what it was, for it was coming from the direction of Galeyville, which was where Curly Bill Graham had hung out since the Earps had chased him from Tombstone.

A group of riders—that much was sure; and larruping as if they had business. They were travelling almighty fast for the heat of the day; but Taisy thought this not too unusual, for that was the way lots of these cowpunchers rode; the most trivial journey was a life-and-death matter were one to judge by the speed they put into it.

But it was some time before she could see them sufficiently plainly to make out individual faces. And when she did her own cheeks paled, and she stared toward the horsemen incredulously. For there in the lead rode Curly Bill Graham with Misery right alongside him!

And then Taisy got a greater shock. For next in the line was Dude Fenner!

She ran out into the trail to meet them, and Misery pulled off his big Stetson hat.

"Why, good evenin', ma'am," he said politely. "And how is your father? Feeling well,

I trust." Then he held up his hand and the caravan stopped; and flashing his grin, Misery said with a flourish:

"I'd like to present Bill Graham, ma'am. He's not fit acquaintance for any lady, I'll grant; but you want to take a good look at him. He's reforming, he says—goin' to get religion an' walk a chalk-line in the future. He's givin' up his hell-tearin' ways an' most of his evil companions. He's seen the light, Bill has, an' he's mendin' his ways. Don't be mindin' his scowl, ma'am—it ain't that he's mad—just embarrassed."

Taisy stood tongue-tied before the burly glowering outlaw that all Arizona was scared of. She wanted to tell the man she was glad he had given up his stage-robbing ways and that she, for one, would not hold his past life against him. But he looked so wickedly villainous she was frightened and could not have spoken to save herself.

But Misery seemed to understand. He said:

"Shucks, now, Miz' Taisy, ma'am. He's just a plain fella like all of us—why, you've no idea! He'd give the very shirt off his back was you to need it more than he did! Gossip has got old Bill all wrong; he's plumb gentle as Mary's lamb, ma'am. An' here's Dude

Fenner, too—fair bubblin' over with the milk o' kindness. An' this here is Judge Burnett, ma'am, both a scholar and a gentleman—"

"I'm proud to know you, ma'am," the Judge said, and dragged off his hat with quaint courtesy; though somehow he managed to keep the shotgun that was in his lap stiffly pointed in Curly Bill's direction.

"An' this here fat boy," Misery said, "owns up to the name of Ballard. He's a horse thief, ma'am, but he's done reformed. Like Curly here, he's seen the error of his ways and has sworn to be a Christian. I'm sorry yo' father ain't around. I'm sure 'twould make him feel good to know that all of us here has made up our minds to make this a better community. The Judge here is a Justice of the Peace, and he's agreed to hold reg'lar services each Sunday in the meetin' house till we can get a preacher from Tombstone."

"Why, how wonderful!" Taisy exclaimed; and Misery had the grace to blush at the radiant smile she flashed him.

"Well," he said, "guess we'll have to be sayin' so long now. We got to hurry or we're goin' to be late for the weddin'—"

"The wedding?" Taisy gasped.

"Sure—hadn't you heard? The Dude here—Mister Fenner, you know—is gettin' married to-day. Yep! Him an' Miz Julia Flystrom are henceforth goin' to tackle life double harness."

Taisy gave the Dude a peculiar look. Then she said with distant politeness:

"Well, isn't that splendid. I'm sure I wish them all the world's luck."

The Dude scowled fit to break his nutcrackers and was about to let fly a vigorous denial when Jones nudged him with his elbow and said:

"Well, we got to be goin'. Give my regards to yo' father, ma'am."

Then they rode off in a boil of dust.

Chapter 10

As they got out of the girl's hearing, the Dude cut loose quickly like a twister. He damned Misery up one side and down the other and then started in all over again. But finally Jones rode alongside and cut Fenner's cussing short.

"Far as I'm concerned, you can orate for the rest of yo natural," he said. "But the facts remains facts just the same. I'll have no Fenner playin' fast an' loose with a nice girl like Julie Flystrom, nor making that dear white-haired old lady a-cry her pore old eyes out. Not for the likes o' *you,* by grab—an' you can roll that up with yo' Durham! when you start playin' barnyard games in the hay—"

"Oh, ho!" said Curly Bill, grinning. *"So thats* what he's been up to, is it?"

He loosed a long hearty guffaw. In fact, it seemed to tickle him so you'd have thought he must have crossed off the score he had got tacked up against Misery. Perhaps that was what he wanted though; for Bill Graham was a smooth one and no kind of guy to pin his heart on his sleeve.

But Misery gave him not even a look; he kept grim eyes fixed on the Dude.

"Whether you like it or not," he told the Dude, "you're goin' through with this— savvy? An' you're goin' to treat Julie plumb like you meant it or you'll get that slick hair-comb done over. I'm not goin' to fool with you, Mister; you better heed what I'm tellin' you."

"When you get to the Flystroms, you see that you act mighty overjoyed at the prospect that's brought you out there. Introduce these gents like they're friends of yours, an' treat Mother Flystrom respectful. You've come to marry Miz' Julie an' you've brought Judge Burnett for the purpose. An' here's one thing you better remember, sonny—not to take *no* for a answer. Next time I stop by the Flystroms I'll expect to hear you are wedded."

Curly Bill said, "Ain't you goin' to see the bride give away?"

"It'll be the lastin' regret of my life, I expect, but unfortunately I'll not be able to. The—er—pressure of business matters—" He waved a hand vaguely and let the rest trail off.

But he saw the quick glint in Dude Fenner's eye, and he didn't need any telescope to guess what the Dude was thinking. He said:

"Don't go entertainin' any wild ideas. The Judge here an' Mister Ballard will be right on hand to see you off proper. They ain't got no confetti, I'm scared, but they'll see that the knot's tied. So if you've got any notion of welshin' out you better get shucked of it pronto. I shan't be very far away, an' if you don't want to be mistook for a sieve you better keep strict to the schedule."

Hate shone bright in the Dude's weasel glance, but he said no more till the Flystrom's shack was seen in the yonder distance. Then he hauled up his horse square in front of Jones' bronc and his left hand brought out his wallet.

"This joke has gone far enough," he snarled. "Go on—name your price! How much you askin' for callin' this off?"

Jones' lip curled contemptuously. Then his eyes got hard as agate.

"It ain't *bein'* called off—an' it ain't no joke. If you think it is, you just try yo' luck an' see how far it'll take you! I'm goin' to lay up here on the rimrock an' watch you across a rifle. An' the first little slip you make, by grab, will sure as heck be yo' last one!"

"I'm goin' to kill you for this if it's the last thing I do!"

"Go on, you worm. Git goin'," Jones said.

Like a whipped cur, the Dude went.

Jones watched till they reached the cabin; then he reined his horse back toward the Galeyville trail and whistled a gay little tune as he rode, for he felt pretty good about this thing. It was, in a manner of speaking, knocking two birds down with a single stone—knocking several down, far as that went. The Dude's marriage took care of a lot of loose ends.

First and foremost it made an honest woman of Julie, and would stop the clack of the old lady's tongue—which was worth all it cost in itself! Then it evened up some of his score with the Dude, and that was quite proper likewise. Moreover, it removed the menace of the Dude's fine manners from Taisy Crawford's vicinity; the Dude wouldn't get very far with Miss Taisy after he was married to Julie! And last—and most important of all—it preserved the Fenner honour. So Jones rode grinning up the Galeyville trail and sang with a lusty vigour.

He would have stuck around to see the fun but for the embarrassment his presence might bring to Miss Julie. She must never guess that the Dude's offer of marriage was anything but voluntary. And Jones being present might have called up some doubts. With him absent, it should go off like clockwork.

The urgent business he had given as an excuse for his not going along was a white lie he felt no shame for. Like the claim he had made he would watch from the rimrock with his big Sharps trained on the cabin. *That* had been to ensure the Dude's compliance, and to protect the Judge and Ballard from subsequent reprisal from Curly Bill

Graham and his six-shooters. Curly Bill wouldn't get obstreperous while he figured he was under Jones' rifle!

But actually Jones had no place to go, for he couldn't well stop by the Crawfords'. Not after telling Taisy he was going to the wedding and was *ben-amigos* with Fenner!

He decided to lope back to Galeyville. He needed some cartridges anyhow, and now was a good time to get them before Curly Bill got back. He sure didn't aim to be around when that happened. Bill wasn't fooling *him* any, for all his large show of good humour. Bill was mad as hops, and Misery was well aware his good luck couldn't hold forever. Next time he and Graham met up there was likely to be fireworks—and plenty!

It was nearly ten in the evening when he rode into Galeyville's street. John Galey's smelter was going full blast, fogging the night with its awful stench, and the barroom doors were wide open.

Misery racked Hawswell's horse in front of McConaghey's and strolled on in with the crowd of red-shirted miners who were making the rounds of the town. Already the place was packed forty deep, and the roulette rattle and chuckaluck games vied with men's oaths and loud laughter. Then a bull-throated miner recognized him and let out a joyous hail.

"Look yere, boys! Lookit who's with us! Sure he's the whippoorwill took Curly Bill Graham outa Babcock's this mornin'. Egad, what a sight! Let's give 'im three rousin' cheers, boys!"

Amid much laughter, the cheers were given, and they all crowded up and slapped Misery's back and told him what a great guy he was. And Misery laughed with them good-naturedly; but to all their questions he turned a deaf ear.

"I got no more idea where Bill is now than you have," he said, and stuck to it.

They didn't believe him, of course, and a lot of them winked and passed broad grins around; but Jones was not to be drawn out. What he wanted, mostly, was to buy his cartridges and get out of town; and he wished he hadn't come in here. But the crowd wouldn't hear of him leaving. They lugged him up to the bar with great oaths and they all insisted on treating him.

Round after round of drinks was set up and, though Misery wanted no drinks at all, to refuse would be to insult his hosts. So he gave in with what grace he could muster and gingerly downed the first five or ten rounds; after that he forgot all his caution.

"Fill 'em up!" he said. "Set 'em up all 'round!"

That started the drunk they date time from. There never was a drinking bout like it; it pulled most of the trade from the town's other dives, and when McConaghey reluctantly closed up at four the next morning there was not a drop left in his bottles.

Curly Bill Graham rode back into town while the Big Spree was in the flower of its progress. But he kept plumb away from McConaghey's bar, and for a while he stayed clear of Babcock's.

He knew what he was about, did Graham; and he wasn't aiming to advertise. He got hold of Petro Petralgo, and together they went and hunted up an apothecary and taxidermist Petralgo knew of who was part Yaqui and could be easily impressed with the sinister suggestion of a flourished .44.

The old man was in bed, but he got up in a hurry when Curly Bill hauled out his smoke-pole. Shaking and chattering and very much of a lather in his anxiety to please the bad men, he undid his chains and padlocks, threw open the creaking door and invited them in.

The place smelled musty and strange, and Curly Bill turned up his nose at the litter of cobwebs and trash with which the old scoundrel surrounded himself. But Petralgo had been there before and paid little heed to the queer assortment of vials and retorts which littered the long crowded work-bench that served the old man for a table.

The rattle of dusty weeds suspended by twine from the rafters startled Curly Bill, and he cursed when he saw what had scared him.

The wrinkled old herb-mixer shivered when Graham's evil eye fell on him, and Petralgo said, pointing to a bottle of amber-coloured liquid, "How much?"

The old man looked, and his death-pale face went paler.

"A-a-ai-hé!" he said, and made the sign of the Cross. "Santa Maria, señor! Recall the proverb: If you are not to eat the stew, mind not how it be cooked." And he spread his hands in a way that indicated all talk on the subject was finished.

But Petralgo was a persistent man, and he put a finger alongside his nose and gave the old man a sly wink. Then he said again, more knowledgeably:

"For the bottle, señor—how much?"

A plain fear twisted the alchemist's mouth (for among many other things he was also that); then his eyes grew suddenly narrowed with guile.

"Bless me!" he smiled and, lifting a knife from the work-bench, he sliced off a lock of his hair. With Petralgo looking uneasily on, he rolled the hair up in the palms of his hands and, with the hands squeezed together, blew on it. After which he sprinkled it around him while he mumbled some abracadabra.

But, suspicious as he was of these strange antics, Petralgo was not to be put off.

"The bottle," he muttered, and laid hand to his pistol.

"As for the bottle, señor—it is yours for the asking."

"For the bottle itself I care nothing!" snapped Petralgo, and Curly Bill nodded, scowling. "This gentleman with me is a friend to the poor; he would purchase the bottle's contents."

"A-a-ai-hé! He would make them comfortable, perhaps." The old man grinned at them slyly, then mumbled some dark incantation.

"Enough of that!" snarled Petralgo in a

rush of furious Spanish oaths. "We are in a hurry, this gentleman and I. While the grass is growing the horse may famish! We will pay you well—but look you, hombre, and mark it well: One word of this and your coffin is started. Be quick now. Wrap up the bottle for His Excellency."

The old man dragged the cap from his head and bowed as if Bill Graham were governor-general to all of the Yaquis. He said:

"Names count less than the purse, God knows; but the bottle's contents are not for sale. Not even for a King's ransom could I sell it, señors. The Yaqui laws forbid it—"

"To hell with the laws!" Curly Bill growled, impatient. And Petralgo said with a roll of his eyes, "Do you know who this *don coballero* is, fellow?"

But the old man shook his head doggedly.

"Not even if it were His Holiness, the Pope, would I dare part with what you ask for. I—"

"Ten thousand devils!" Petralgo snapped in a rage, and jabbed his gun at the old man's belly. "Wrap the bottle instantaneous!"

"Alack and alas, señor—but it is the *acid!*" the alchemist wailed. "The oh-so-potent acid that will—"

"We know what it is!" Petralgo snapped. "Wrap it up and be nimble or—"

But Curly Bill was fed up with these Latin amenities. He knew a surer and swifter way with such fools. With a ripped-out oath he leaned suddenly forward and dropped the old man with his gun barrel.

"Power of God!" cried Petralgo, crossing himself. "You have killed the old witch—"

"What of it?" Bill said, and reached up and brought down the bottle. "We've got the damn acid, an' that's what we came here for, ain't it? Then quit jibberin' an' let's get the hell outa here!"

It was some two hours later when Petralgo, by himself, knocked at the shack in the Turkey Creek bottoms where lived Sligo, one of Babcock's barmen. The hour was late—or early, if you choose—being half past two in the morning, and the shack was dark; but Sligo, whose conscience packed considerable weight, was known to be easily wakened.

At his second knock Petralgo heard the slither of movement and the furtive pad of bare feet on stamped ground; and Sligo's husky wheeze demanded knowledge of the visitor's identity.

"Who the devil d'you think's out here? The Mayor of Albuquerque? Open up, you fool, or Curly Beel will have you staked out on an ant hill." And to make sure of haste, Petralgo kicked at the door in a passion.

Sligo pulled him in in alarm.

"D'you have to tell the whole town about it?"

He was a squint-eyed, fat little worm of a man who would do anything for a profit—a pariah even among bandits.

"Make a light," Petralgo growled. "Must an honest man talk in the darkness?"

Sligo muttered, but he lit the oil lamp that was bracketed over the table. Then he dragged up a chair for his visitor; but Petralgo, eyeing it suspiciously, said:

"What I've got to say won't take that long."

He took a squat package from under his arm and set it gingerly down on the table.

"You know that one called Misery Jones?"

Sligo nodded cautiously.

"Listen close then," Petralgo bade him, and unwrapped his package, disclosing a small bottle of amber-coloured liquid. "This is for Jones. He is make the beeg drunk tonight. Tomorrow when he wakes up his head will be loco-haywire. He will feel like the hell and will come to the Señor Nick's for w'at you call the 'hair of the dog'—you understand?"

Sligo grunted.

"But why Babcock's? There's other places in—"

"Be still, fool! I tell you he will come to the Señor Nick's," declared Petralgo gruffly. "Now bend the ear. W'en this gringo comes in for the drink I will be there. I will greet him like the lost brother, an' I will bring him up to the bar. I will say, 'The best is none too good for my great friend, Señor Misery,' and you will set out a bottle of whisky in which you have mixed the contents of this bottle—savvy?"

"No," Sligo growled, "But I can see right now this bird is goin' to be suspicious—"

"Fool! How can he be suspicious when the drink you serve me is the last one in the bottle it comes out of? And you had best see that it *is* the last one—an' that none of this stuff is in it! Comprehend? Pay heed, then. The bottle from which you serve my so-good friend, this gringo, must be a new one, to all intents unopened. But if you like your hide the way it is you will see to it that all the liquid in this bottle"—Petralgo paused to tap the bottle he had set on the table—"is also in the one from which this gringo drinks.

"And for all this dangerous business I get—what?" asked Sligo craftily.

"You'll be paid, never fear."

"You bet! And in advance. Right now! Or you an' me don't do business, friend."

"*Carramba!* A thousand devils! Is it that you doubt my word?" demanded Petralgo with an evil scowl.

Sligo hastened to reassure him.

"But accidents can happen. If it's all the same to you I'll take my pay in advance."

"I haven't the money with me—"

"Well, that's too bad. Better take your bottle to someone else," Sligo said with a shrug; and his fat face showed a cunning smile that made Petralgo gnash his teeth, and he reached for his knife as though of half a mind to slit the barman's gullet.

But Sligo leered and held his ground. He folded his arms across his chest and scratched his back on the door frame.

"Take it or leave it," he said, chuckling; and with a curse Petralgo brought out his poke.

"Don't bother yourself with counting it, friend," murmured Sligo, breaking the back of the tall Mex's profanity. "I'll take that poke just the way she lays."

"He that will ape the hog—"

"Save your breath. I know all them old saws backwards," grinned Sligo, "an' I ain't impressed by any of 'em. If you want me to do this little trick for you, the price is as stated—no discounts."

Chapter 11

When Jones woke up he was out in a bottle-filled alley with a large tin can for a pillow and with trash piles heaped all around him. It was in no sense a proper environment for a man of his crusading talents to rise and shine upon. But Misery wasn't doing any shining right then, nor did he immediately get himself upright. He groaned several times quite dismally and gave his surroundings a bleary-eyed stare. Then he groaned again and felt his head and, closing his eyes, loosed an oath. It was a long way from being cheerful.

He swore again when he thought of Taisy, and what she would say should she hear of it. It would not be complimentary.

"Oh, me!" he muttered drearily; and propped himself up on an elbow.

He looked merry as an undertaker and felt

like a man who had ridden a cyclone with the bridle off. If he ever took another drop—

He paused to loose another groan, and decided not to swear off quite yet, because if he ever needed anything, right now was the time, and what he stood in need of was another glass of the same—more hair of the dog that bit him. Otherwise there was no telling how long his misery would be with him.

One thing was sure: He'd better get afoot and hie himself out of this alley. It was no fit place for a champion of right and virtue to be found in, and he would sure like to wring the slat-eyed gizzard of the buzzard who had dumped him here as if he were a bucket of swill or something. He would like, in fact, to kick John Barleycorn right in the seat of his britches!

He got a wobbly knee braced under him and shoved himself to his feet. Dawn's fresh light was a faint pink haze along the eastern horizon. Jones had no notion where he was, except that it was in Galeyville; but he had an uneasy feeling that he should have been some place else.

He leaned against the frame wall of a building and tried to take stock of the damage. Seemed as if he still had his guns and there didn't seem to be any bones broken, so he guessed he hadn't been in a fight. But he felt like hell with the blower on, and he wondered if there were any joints open where he could fresh himself up with a drink.

He staggered out of the alley and looked up and down the street. Yep—this was Galeyville, all right; but the place sure looked plumb deserted. There were a couple of tied broncs in front of Babcock's bar; so it looked as if Nick, anyway, were open. But the rest of the town was closed up tight. He wondered where his horse had gone—that swell black he had lifted from Hawswell. He peered all around, but it wasn't in sight. Maybe Hawswell had come and got him.

But no, that didn't make sense. For Hawswell would never ride off without wreaking some kind of revenge, he was sure. For the guy wasn't that kind of Christian.

"Woe is me!" he muttered, and began to go through his pockets.

Suddenly he cursed in a passion. Someone had rolled him surer than sin; they hadn't left him even a pluggd nickel! All that folding money he had bulled away from Bill Graham was gone; and he started for McConaghey's hotfoot.

But the place was closed and locked up

tight and there was a "For Rent" sign on the door.

Misery glared. Then he looked for his guns and was some relieved when he found he still had them. Maybe McConaghey was not to blame for his plight after all. It was just possible somebody else had rolled him and then dumped him out in that alley.

Then another thought struck him, and he reached for the gun on his hip. He broke it open, and the morning light glinted back from all five shell rims.

He was putting the gun away again when another notion struck him and he shook the shells out of the cylinder. And then he cursed in a fury. It was a put-up job all right! Some polecat was out to do him dirt, and he didn't have to search his mind very long to slap a name on the critter.

"Curly Bill, by grab!" he exploded. "Or I'm a centipede's uncle!"

He glared towards Nick Babcock's angrily, though neither of the broncs was Bill's. He eyed the shells in his hand again, then hurled them through McConaghey's window and with a black scowl struck out for Nick Babcock's bar, stuffing fresh loads in his gun. For all the cartridges he had just heaved away had had their leads extracted!

He forgot his aching head in his wrath—even forgot what Taisy might say. But ere he reach Nick Babcock's bar some modicum of caution returned to him to slow the pace of his forward charge. It would be sheerest folly to go whamming into Babcock's place without knowing what he was up against. If Curly Bill was back of this, he'd probably have the place jammed solid with gunslicks; and all they'd need to start burning powder would be just the merest sight of him!

So he hauled off and peered around a bit.

Not that it did much good; it didn't advance his knowledge a particle. There was just so much to be seen and not a smidgin more. Two tired broncs were tied in front of the place. One of them was Petralgo's horse; the other was a strange caballo he didn't recall having seen before.

By this time, though, a deal of Misery's steam had disappeared and he wasn't feeling quite so warlike. The need of a drink was uppermost in his mind again; and his aches had come back increased threefold.

He walked clean around Nick Babcock's place. But there were no saddled horses cached out back, nor down in the Turkey Creek bottoms. The smoke curling up from Galey's stamp mill was the only sign of life in sight. Misery hitched his six-shooter around for quick reaching and parted the batwing doors.

The place was completely empty save for Petralgo, a pasty-faced barkeep and a drunk raucously snoring it off at a table far back in a corner. There wasn't even one of Nick's girls hanging around to pry the boys loose from their cash. Misery took another, closer look at the drunk and unleashed a disgusted whistle. It was Short Beer Ballard—and the fellow was piped to the gills.

Being afoot himself, Mister Jones felt very virtuous and grinned when Petralgo greeted him.

"Buenos dias, señor," Petro said with a quick, bright flash of the teeth; and Misery, not to be outdone in politeness by a mealy-mouthed stage-boot robber, answered:

"Top of the morning to you—that was a fine large time we had last night. How come McConaghey's sellin'out?"

"No can get the tequila—no polque, maguey, whisky—no nothing! *Carramba!* All sold out!"

"Well, he can get more in, can't he?"

"Ah! Not that one, señor. Nick Babcock ees the beeg boss here—*seguro si,* señor! If Senor Babcock say, 'No bring the barrels—no bottles for Senor McConaghey!' no barrels, no bottles come! *Sabe Dios.* W'at use for stay open, eh?"

"Hmmm. Freezin' out competition, eh? A lousy Philistine trick, by grab! What kind of a Christian *is* he?"

"*Quien sabe, señor?* But have a care with the talk—even the walls have the ears in Galeyville, and Senor Babcock is Curly Beel's friend."

"An' *your* friend, too, by jingoes!" Misery growled, and squinted up his eyes belligerently.

But Petralgo shrugged it off. "You have had the *sayuno,* señor?"

"Huh? Oh—breakfast! No, I ain't et yet. A drink's what I come in here for. I gotta wash the bad taste from my mouth."

"The morning after, eh?" Petralgo laughed. "Come—have a dreenk on me."

Misery eyed him suspiciously; for the last time he'd talked with this fellow, Petralgo had not been so friendly.

But he was showing all smiles and good nature now. Butter wouldn't melt in his mouth, Misery thought. But a drink was a

126

drink, and Jones needed one, so he followed Petralgo up to the bar.

The swivel-eyed barkeep set out a bottle with hardly a swallow left in it. He had the grace to flush under Misery's dark stare; but Petralgo said smoothly:

"*Ai!* Power above! What treatment is this for a *don caballero?* Set out a fresh one, fool! The best in the house for my friend."

Jones scowled as the barkeep reached down a fresh bottle from a stack of the same on the back bar. Some warning impulse surged through him. But his aches were many and the effects of the last night's carousal had slowed up his wits considerably. Still uneasy, he shrugged, broke the neck from the bottle like a true *caballero* and poured himself out a good measure.

"Your health, señor!" Petralgo cried; and Misery, hoisting his glass, went stiff.

For there in the bar's mirror the face of Curly Bill showed at the batwings. And the grin that flashed on Curly Bill's teeth was not to be found in his stare. There was a wicked glitter in the outlaw boss' eyes; and Misery Jones cut loose of his glass and with a quick spin yanked out his belt gun.

With a wild shriek Petralgo reeled back, hands clawed to his eyes, as Jones' glass and

Jones' drink took him square in the face; and Curly Bill, startled, leaped clear of Nick's porch to the trip-hammer beat of Jones' gun.

Every move Misery made was instinctive; and, flushed with success, he let out a roar and jumped his lean frame to the batwings.

"Come back here, you sidewindin' Judas!" he howled; but Graham had had all that he wanted. Misery saw him sprinting full-tilt down the street. Then he vanished up an alley in a cloud of dust; and Misery hooted derisively.

"Hoo, hoo!" he jeered. "The curly wolf of Galeyville has done gone to hunt him a hole!"

Chapter 12

Just the same, Misery thought when he paused to cool off, that tough Curly Bill had been out to lift his scalp, sure enough; and would be a heap likely to try it again. This was no time to pick any daisies.

Nor did he! He piled into Petralgo's saddle and used his big spurs to advantage. He left Galeyville to the wolves that liked it and lit a quick shuck for the San Simon

Pass; and he went tearing through it like a twister.

It was getting well into the afternoon's shank when he came in sight of the Crawfords' holdings, and Petralgo's horse was well covered with lather when he pulled up in front of the claimshack.

But Taisy had seen him coming; and there she came, running to meet him with a quick, glad light in her eyes.

Then she noticed his look and she stared at his horse, and abruptly her face went sober. In a shocked tone of voice she said:

"Why, Misery!"

"It's all that durn Bill Graham again! The whoppy-jawed—"

"But I thought you said he'd reformed—" cried Taisy; and Misery's scowl went uneasy.

"The chipmunk fooled me—or if he did, he's backslid. Jest lyin', I reckon. He's a hound-low, sneakin' polecat thief that would steal the pennies out of a blind man's cup! Never let him get within gunshot of this place or your life won't be worth a plugged nickel!"

Taisy stood silent, her face plainly showing the upset state of her emotions. She said suddenly:

"But *that* isn't your horse! Where's that fine black saddler you were riding yesterday when you went to Dude Fenner's wedding?"

"Some sidewinder stole 'im—but I'll get 'im back," growled Misery darkly; and just then Morgan Crawford came out and was reaching to pump Jones' hand when Taisy said, coming close:

"How did your new vest get all torn like that?" And before he could think up an alibi, she said, "Misery! You've been drinking!" A rush of colour spread over his face. "Oh, Misery!" Taisy burst out reproachfully.

Misery muttered under his breath, but he wouldn't meet her eye.

"Well—ahem!" Morgan Crawford said charitably. "The best of men need a drink sometimes. . . ."

Misery gave him a grateful glance.

"It was that danged weddin'," he told them. "There was a big celebration in town last night an' I downed a sight more than I figured to."

Which was the truth without any varnish; and Misery shot her a look to see how Taisy was taking it. But it was pretty clear she didn't hold with liquor, for she looked at Jones uncomfortably and she shook her copper locks sadly.

Misery made haste to change the subject, for he did not like to have his shortcomings harped on, and he had heard every bit he cared to hear about the Big Drunk at Galeyville. He said, "Has the Dude called 'round?" and Crawford peered off toward the ridge rather queerly.

Misery whirled a quick look at it; but all he could see was the ridge and the trees and the way the wind blew through the grasses, so he guessed it was something that was in the man's mind that made Crawford act so daunsy.

"You seem kind of put out, suh," Jones ventured. "What's the matter? Don't you care for the Dude's selection?"

"Uh—eh?" Crawford peered at him absentmindedly. "Oh—you mean the Dude's choice in matrimony. Why, yes; I think Mister Fenner may have hit upon a very—er—able—ah—helpmate. Did I understand Taisy to tell me you—ah—"

"Go right ahead, suh. Spit it out," Misery encouraged. "Get it off yo' chest an' you'll feel better."

"Hmm—yes. Well, I was under the impression, Mister Jones, that you gave Taisy to understand Mister Fenner's wedding was scheduled for—umm—ah—yesterday."

"What about it?"

"Why—umm—I'm not sure I quite know how to put it, but—"

"Well, *I* do!" declared Taisy vehemently. "I thought it queer the Dude didn't talk much yesterday—but it's plain enough to folks *now*, I guess! He never intended to marry Julie Flystrom."

"He—*what's that!*" Misery roared in a fury. "You claim they're not married?"

"Of course they're not—nor ever intended to be!" Taisy cried. "Oh, Misery! How *could* you do it? How *could* you tell me such lies?"

Misery looked startled; then his mind started working, and he guessed this was some of the old man's doings and stuck out his chin at Crawford.

"Where'd you get this stuff?" he demanded. "Did the Dude *tell* you he wasn't married?" And he screwed up his eyes so belligerently Morgan Crawford backed off in alarm.

"Why—uh—er—*no*," Taisy's father admitted. "I haven't seen Mister Fenner. But I passed the Flystroms' claimshack this noon, and there sat Julie out on the stoop crying like her poor heart would break. She was all slumped over, with her face all puffed up and a rifle all loaded and ready. I thought for a second she meant to shoot me; but it was Mister Fenner she was waiting for."

Misery cursed like a mule-skinning private. He forgot all about being a gentleman.

"It's all the fault of that stinkin' Bill Graham!" he shouted. "I never should ought to have trusted him! That's just what a fella gets when he tries to treat skunks like a gentleman! I ort to knocked his brains out!"

He might have said more—a great deal more; only just then, with a shocked kind of gasp and with cheeks gone scarlet as beet juice, Taisy clapped hands to her ears and incontinently fled to the house.

That was when Jones really opened up. He kicked the lid off his cusswords and described Curly Bill and his forbears in words handed down from the Saxons.

Morgan Crawford stood dumbfounded, like a mackerel dumped in a skillet. A kind of Horatio-at-the-bridge look got in his stare, and it seemed as if he wanted to say something, but Misery never gave him a chance.

"The golrammed whoppy-jawed sidewinder!" he snarled, and shook his fist in a fury—his left one, because he hadn't had that much use of his right since Sheridan had come down the Shenandoah. "The fish-bellied shorthorn! *I'll* show 'im! The damned baboon-faced prairie dog! I'll kick his pants up 'round his ears till they fit so tight they'll choke 'im to death! He can't run no blazer like that on *me!*"

Crawford's glance was getting pretty nervous, and the way he was twisting his vest flaps up proved Taisy was in for an ironing. But Jones wouldn't let him say anything.

"Not marry 'er, eh? *I'll* learn him!" he shouted and Crawford guessed they could hear him to Payson. "The high-stomachs pup! The mealy-mouthed hound!" And he loosed a wild round of army-camp oaths; then he waggled a finger beneath Crawford's nose. *"I'll* show the swiveleyed polecat! The two-by-four hole in a doughnut! Who does he think he *is,* by grab—goin' 'round seducin' these nester girls! Reg'lar Don Jo-An!" he snarled, and jumped his voice to the top of Fish Canyon. "Jest wait'll I get my hands on him! I'll teach him to drag the Fenner name—"

"But, Mister Jones! Now really—" Crawford began; but Misery held his hand up, listening. And Crawford said through the hoof sound, "I've been trying to tell you for the past five minutes! There's a bunch of riders fogging over that ridge, and I think that's Curly Bill leading them—"

But Misery was no longer listening. He took one look and left like a streak of forked lightning.

Chapter 13

It was Graham, all right, and he wasn't picking posies. There'd be plenty of those put on Misery's grave if Curly Bill ever got hold of him. That one quick look had told Misery that much; and he wasn't waiting for details. He pulled out on the instant and did not look back for six miles. When he did swing a quick look backwards he found Graham hard on his heels.

It was plain enough now why Bill Graham had run off when Misery had splintered Nick's batwings. He'd gone to get help— and he sure got it. There were fifteen guys in that bunch chasing Jones, and every man of them packed a rifle. And they were plenty willing to use them, as a sudden fusillade gave warning. Twigs from the overhead branches dropped down Jones' neck; both heels were shot from his boots and his hat rim fell round his ears like a halo as a salvo of lead took the crown right out of it and cut off some locks of his hair in its passing. It was plain those fellows weren't fooling!

Misery crouched low down on his borrowed bronc's neck and plied both his spurs with vigour. But though Petralgo's horse gave its entire speed, and its heart and its soul into the bargain, Misery didn't gain more than a couple of scant yards, and Graham's tough crew kept on shooting.

It could only be a question of time before Graham's aim was accomplished; unless, Misery muttered to himself with a curse, he could find some hole to crawl into.

Then abruptly he thought of the Flystroms. If he could only make that tumbledown line-rider's shack there was just a bare chance he could hold them off—or at least delay the massacre.

He whirled Petralgo's horse hard to the left and lined him off through a motte of trees that was cut across by a gully. Straight down the cut-bank he slammed the big bronc and then yanked him hard back on his haunches.

Grabbing his rifle, he jumped from the saddle and went clambering up the shaley slope till he came to a big red boulder that offered some cover and also a chancy view of the trail. The first look he took showed Graham's bunch entering the trees. They were coming hellity-larrup.

Misery wasted no time. He clapped up his rifle and let fly at once, and saw a guy pitch from his saddle. He fired twice more before Graham's crowd took to the brush.

"Movin' day!" Misery muttered, and slid down the bank in a dust cloud. Petralgo's bronc was just fixing to run off; but Misery leaped, got a grip on its tail and hauled himself over the cantle. For seconds, as he topped the arroyo's farther bank, the air was filled with the shrill whine of flying lead; then he was out of it, the slope of the land serving to hide him till Curly Bill's smokeroos could manage to cross the gully.

Meantime, Misery was making good use of those precious minutes to increase his lead; by the time Graham's outfit topped the dry wash of the eastern wall Petralgo's bronc had taken Misery out of sight, and considerable time was lost picking up his trail again.

But Misery was not lingering. He was spurring madly through a series of crisscross barrancas which he hoped would bring him out at the old line-rider's shack on

Fenner range where the Flystroms were try-ing their hands at sodbusting.

And so, in time, it did; but when he sighted the haywire spread Petralgo's horse was stumbling.

Misery rode the winded bronc straight past the Flystroms' cabin, and not until he had the critter heading up a ridge did Misery quit the saddle. The horse was ready to quit likewise, but Misery slapped him hard on the rump, and the lathered equine staggered over the hill and out of sight.

Not until he was sure the horse *was* out of sight did Misery sprint for the claim-shack, and then he made for the back door. He saw nobody in sight, neither Graham's tough bucks nor either of the Flystroms. He saw a patch of fresh turned earth some forty yards back of the shack, though, that seemed to augur Julie had got to work on her plant-ing.

He rapped on the door, but didn't await any answer. He shoved it open and strode on in; and there was Julie at the kitchen table with her face buried in her arms.

He thought at first she'd been sobbing. But Julie was made of sterner stuff, and it took a good deal to wring any tears out of *her* eyes. Perhaps she had been crying at that, for her cheeks looked kind of flushed and swollen; but her eyes were sullen, defiant, when she lifted her head off the table.

"You can go—she said, and suddenly stopped, her dark eyes springing wide and startled as she saw who it was in the doorway.

"Why, Mister *Jones!*" she cried, surging up. "What in the world—you've been hurt!" she cried; and rushed straight away for the dipper and bucket.

She plopped them down on the table and commenced ripping up a flour-sack towel.

"Peel off that shirt right away."

"Now, ma'am," Jones said, somewhat embarrassed, "don't you be takin' on so—it ain't nothin' but a measly ol' scratch; an' anyway—"

"Peel off that shirt!" Julie snapped at him. "Unless," she told him tartly, "it's that you're afraid for a girl to see you! Lord! you needn't mind *me,*" she declared, with a dark flash of eyes; "my mother could have told you I *know all* about men folk!"

But while the piquant face framed in corn silk curls showed darkly sullen and resentful, the girl's deft fingers were busy; and almost before Misery knew what was happening she had whisked him out of his shirt.

It was only a flesh wound, but ugly and ragged; and Misery figured he was almighty lucky to have got clear with his life. The way Graham's gunslicks had been pumping lead had been enough to turn a man's hair grey. It was his left hand, too—his good hand. The bullet had gone in just under the elbow and come out on the other side over the wrist. No bones had been broken, but it hurt like hell, and he'd lost, Julie told him, a sight more blood than a man in his fix could afford to.

"I'll sure lose a sight more than blood, ma'am, if I don't find some safe place to hide out in."

"What happened? Did you get in a fight?"

"I don't know if you'd call it a fight, ma'am; but it was kind of hot while it lasted. And it's like to resume most any time. Curly Bill's crowd is after me—"

"*Shh!*" she cried, going tense, head canted. "Listen!"

Misery nodded.

"Yeah—that's them all right. They wasn't far behind me. I was scared they'd pick up my trail. I rode right on past here, but—"

"Quick!" Julie said. "They'll search the place sure. I'll go out and swap some—small talk while you slip on Mother's things. You'll find them all hung up in the closet—just pile right into them, cowboy, or—"

"But, ma'am! What will your—"

"Go on!" she cried sharply. "Don't be a ninny!" And here—put your shirt back on; we can't have 'em finding your clothes strewn around!" And snatching up her rifle, she went hurrying out on the porch.

And none too soon. Misery heard Graham's men pulling up outside.

"Did you see a pumpkin-faced jasper go larrupin' by?" Curly Bill's bull-throated road demanded. "A long-geared wart by the name of M. Jones?"

Misery tip-toed into the front room then and did not hear any more for a bit, being too busy slipping into Mrs. Flystrom's old blue house-dress, shawl and little poke bonnet. What Mrs. Flystrom would say were she to return and find him wearing them was something he didn't dwell on.

First things first; and right now the prime consideration, as Julie had pointed out, was escaping Curly Bill's clutches. He didn't know which might prove the worse, Curly Bill's or old Mrs. Flystrom's—but Curly Bill was right on tap and by good luck Mrs. Flystrom wasn't; so Misery piled into her clothes and, shoving his hat-brim down a bootleg, folded his hands in some needle-work and with his six-shooter under it parked in his lap, plopped himself down in the wheel-chair.

Not until he was actually seated, with the old lady's blue dress so pulled down as to hide his boot toes, did Misery realize the significance of Mrs. Flystrom being out of that chair.

"Lor—*dy!*" he groaned, and felt great goose-bumps start to crawling.

The new-turned earth out back of the house, the empty chair and the absence of the old lady herself, when put together in just that fashion, were sure indications of Mrs. Flystrom's whereabouts.

With a hoarser groan, Misery started up. But the approaching sound of Graham's bull-bellow drove him, sweating, down into the chair.

"I'll just make sure," Graham said through his teeth. "Not that I'm doubtin' your veracity, ma'am. But this horse-thievin' Jones is a slippery customer an' he might of slipped in unbeknownst to you."

"But I told you," Julie said, "I saw him cross that ridge over there."

"We'll very soon know," Curly Bill said grim-ly. "Meantime I'll just look over the house."

In he came, puffed up like a grizzly, with his open shirt showing the hair on his chest and with his black, scowling stare swinging around like a mallet.

"Mother," Julie said, "this is Bill Graham. You remember—he was by here yesterday with Mister Dude Fenner—"

Misery half looked around to find the old lady. He stopped just in time. It was he Julie was talking to; *he* was supposed to be old Mrs. Flystrom. He emitted a grunt as he'd heard her do, and kept his head bent as if he were all taken up with his needlework, and prayed mighty fervently. Graham would not peer beneath the hood of his bonnet.

But Curly Bill wasted hardly a look at the frail bent figure in the old wheel chair. He poked in the closet, squeezed all the dresses and, finally satisfied, went out in the kitchen. Misery could hear him stamping about.

Julie stood by the door with her dark eyes mocking.

"He's not in that cookie jar," she said scornfully.

"I didn't think he was," Bill Graham muttered through a mouthful of chewing. "Them's right good cakes, though. We'll take 'em along. The ol' woman make 'em?"

"Of course not. Mother can't hardly get

143

out of her chair," Julie said; and Misery winced, for he was a sight too close to Boot Hill himself to enjoy playing double for a dead woman.

Just the same, his opinion of Julie had risen considerably. She had all her wits about her, that girl had; and he knew she wasn't liking this any better than he was. Quite naturally she was torn with grief over her mother's passing; and no matter what kind of tongue the old lady had had, a person's relations take a lot more off of them than other folks would. Blood was thicker than water any way you measured it.

Bill Graham came clanking his way back again; and Misery's fingers clamped tight around his six-gun under the needlework. For it seemed as if Curly Bill were bound to get wise. Old Mrs. Flystrom had been a great one for exercising her talking talents. Her continued silence was bound to be noticed, if it hadn't already been.

But just then Graham said:

"Mighty sorry to have bothered you yesterday, ma'am. . . ."

And as the quietness deepened it was borne in on Misery that Curly Bill's words had been aimed at him!

Chapter 14

But what could he *do?* If he opened his mouth to do more than grunt, Curly Bill would be on to him like the side of a mountain, and he couldn't continue to sit there like a sphinx!

"What the matter with' er?" Curly Bill said. "Is she *deef*"

"She's not feeling well to-day," Julie said. "And when she don't feel good—Well, really, now that you've proved for yourself that Jones isn't around here, don't you think maybe you'd better go on outside?"

"Humph! I'll go when I'm ready," Graham growled.

And just when Misery had given up all hope and was wondering what kind of harp he'd be expected to play, a horse loped into the yard and a rider's boots hit dirt and somebody yelled:

"Hey—Bill! We found that bronc!" and Curly Bill dashed out of the place with Julie hotfoot after him.

"Well, damn my eyes!" Misery heard Bill snarl. "Where the hell did you locate him?"

"Jest across that ridge off there—it was

Petralgo's horse, all right. Funny thing about that critter . . . . You know, Bill, we found that horse standing with his head 'tween his legs, too dead beat to eat, even. An' there wa'n't no sign of Jones around no-where—no, sir! not one dad-blamed sign!"

Misery, flattened to the wall alongside a window, heard Graham swear. He was mad enough to chew the sights off a six-gun, seemed like. And Misery, taking one brief, rushed squint, saw him glare suspiciously at Julie.

"I'll bet *you* know where the bird has gone to!"

"Don't be foolish!" Julie tossed her head. Then her eyes grew big with wonder. "Do you suppose," she gasped, "he could have jumped off his horse and hid out in the brush some place?"

"Ah—you *women!*" Graham whirled big shoulders savagely. "Did you hunt for tracks?" he snapped at the man.

The fellow just shook his head, baffled.

"We found the horse. Hadn't moved a inch from the time he stopped—which wa'n't over half an hour ago, hardly. But that dang horse-thievin' smokeroo wa'n't any place around. We beat the brush clean back to the ridge—not a sign of 'im—not a track.

If he jumped he must of grabbed for a cloud, cause he sure didn't light on the ground, by grab!"

Graham swore some more. He looked wicked enough to scare a snake away from its young ones. But all his fuming didn't seem to help much. He paused once or twice when he saw Julie smiling and seemed of a mind to smack her. But he didn't; and pretty soon he climbed up into his saddle.

"But I'll get 'im!" he snarled. "You watch my smoke! There ain't nobody can bamboozle Bill Graham that way an' live to do any braggin'! You mark my words: I'll break every bone in his body!"

After Graham's crowd had gone, Julie came in the house and shrugged at Jones philosophically.

"I guess you heard all his ranting. . . . He talks big, but he acts big, too, and you don't want to underestimate him. He nurses hate like an Indian; he'd just as lief cut your heart out as eat—and I guess a lot liefer if the truth was told. You want to watch out for him, Mister. How did you ever get him so riled?"

"Don't ask *me*," Misery grunted wearily. "He just come by it natural, I guess."

"I'd like to ask you something," she said;

and abruptly Misery went watchful. It was something in her tone—in the way she looked as she said it.

He climbed out of Mrs. Flystrom's clothes, sank weakly down on an edge of the bed, and closed his eyes to shut out the pain—but mostly to avoid Miss Julie's sharp look.

"Ask ahead," he muttered. "What is it?"

"Did you send the Dude over here yesterday?"

Misery sat bolt upright.

"I sh'd say not! Where'd yo' git that crazy notion? The Dude an' me ain't speakin' no more. What would I send him over here for?"

Her eyes raked over him searchingly; and suddenly Misery really *felt* weak, and his face got pale as a bedsheet. He didn't like that look in her eye; and he almost wished Bill Graham would come back—anything to create a distraction.

Then Miss Julie rose up in a sudden impatience and took a quick turn around the room.

"There's something darn queer about it anyway," she said. "He came out here yesterday with a whole procession—Curly Bill and two or three other men. He said he wanted to marry me—"

"Who? Curly Bill?"

"No," Julie said. "Dude Fenner"; and she tapped at the floor with her high-heeled boot. "I suppose I am a fool," she said. "Lots of girls would have jumped at the chance of marrying into all that money—"

"You—you turned him down?" Misery managed to gulp.

Julie nodded.

"Oh—I know what you're thinking," she said with curling lips. "But I'm no two-dollar hussy. If I like a man—"

"But I thought you liked Dude Fenner—"

"Not enough to marry him *that* way." Julie's turbulent eyes were scornful. "Somebody put him up to it—he no more wanted to marry me than a jackrabbit would a bullfrog!"

Misery eyed her bewilderedly. "But if he said—"

"Humph! Words!" Julie said, with her lips curling down. "You'd think he was reciting something the teacher had made him memorize. That wasn't the way he talked when— *Never mind!* I feel cheap every time I think of it. Let me see that arm again; I'd better put on a clean bandage. . . ."

The next thing Misery remembered he was

back in the Crawford claimshack again, with its cool white walls and chintz curtains. And there was Taisy at the foot of the bed, and her eyes looked as if she'd been crying. Seemed as if he ought to say something to reassure her—tell her he was comfortable, or something; getting along as well as could be expected, maybe—that was what they said in hospitals.

But ere his lips could shape the words he was off in a moaning sleep again. He rolled and tossed and muttered, and swore wild oaths in his dreaming.

But next time he woke up his head was clearer, and there was Taisy bending over the stove just like the first time he'd come there. And there was her father, over by the water pail, shaving by the little cracked mirror.

Misery guessed he could do with a shave himself; and felt plumb disgusted he was such a bother. Seemed as if he were always bunged up and the Crawfords having to take care of him. It wasn't right for a grown-up man to get bowled over so easily. Seemed as if he didn't have any stamina at all, hardly. He guessed he must be a sissy or something, because he'd only been shot in the arm—and just a flesh wound at that. Lots of guys rode with a leg shot off and didn't think anything about it. Why, after Antietam—

Just then Taisy turned and saw his eyes open. "Oh, Father!" she cried, "He's awake again!" Crawford laid down his razor and came hurrying over, with Taisy fluttering around him.

"How you feelin', son? Think you could take on some nourishment?"

"Suh—them's right pleasant words," Misery said, and managed a wan sort of grin. "I'm downright embarrassed to be so un-handy thisaway."

"Hmmm . . . I suppose you are. Just lay quiet now—relax. Taisy will fix you some broth after a while. You're feeling weak as a kitten, I shouldn't wonder. Got cause to. You've lost a lot of blood, young fellow; a powerful lot—"

"How'd I get here *this* time?"

"Miss Julie came over and brought you."

"Miz' Julie! Why, she couldn't never lift—"

"She did, though brought you in across the front of her saddle. Walked all the way over here leading her horse; had you roped on just like a gold sack. She was scared you were dying and frightened half out of her wits," Crawford said. "Miss Julie is a mighty brave girl—"

But Misery didn't hear any more; he had fainted plumb away again.

It was two days more before he could get up—before, that is, Crawford would *let* him get up; and waiting was the hardest thing Jones could do. He had always been an impatient sort, always jumping around like a hen on a griddle. But Taisy helped him pass the time away; and that was one thing he could do mighty easily—lie there and stare into Taisy's flushed face while they talked about—say, now! What *had* they talked about? Seemed as if they'd always had plenty to say; but for the life of him Misery couldn't remember a bit of it!

Well, he did remember *one* thing. Julie had told her about Dude Fenner's visit; and Taisy had been madder than hops. Not with Julie—nor with the Dude, of course; but with Misery for putting Dude Fenner up to it. She had made him confess every bit of it; and while he was at it, Misery had told her that he was a Fenner, that the Dude was his brother and had refused to recognize him and had driven him away from their door.

Of course Taisy hadn't believed him. She wouldn't accept a word of it, or hear anything bad of Dude Fenner. He was back in her good graces again. Misery guessed he had been seeing her some place, and he gnashed his teeth in a passion; but apparently Taisy had not told the Dude where Misery was, or the Dude would have passed it right on to Bill Graham and Curly Bill would have lifted hell up and shoved a chunk under it. Because he was that kind of a hombre—sick folks and dogs were all one to *him*—he nailed up his hides where he found them.

If Taisy had any inkling of why Misery had wanted to make the Dude marry Julie, she was keeping it to herself. If she guessed the truth, she must have believed Jones Fenner mistaken; for she stuck up for the Dude through hell and high water. It almost soured Misery on women.

Then, on the afternoon before he got up, Crawford came back from a ride up the valley with his pale face grave as an undertaker. Curly Bill, he said, was hunting all through the mountains for someone, swearing to cut his heart out and make the poor fellow eat it.

"And I'm afraid," Crawford said in conclusion, "the fellow he's looking for is you."

Misery had guessed that part right off, and he scowled at his bandage-swathed arm.

Crawford shook his head.

"You wouldn't stand a chance," he said. "Not against a man like Curly Bill Graham. He's chain lightning with a gun. I was over in Tombstone the day he killed Marshal Fred White, and I tell you it was the quickest thing I've ever seen. He's a bad actor, boy— keep away from him."

Misery muttered to himself and thought of a whole heap of things he could do to Bill Graham if only he weren't a cripple.

"Can't you do somethin' about this bad paw of mine? Somebody was tellin' me you was a famous doc in Chicago."

Crawford smiled sadly.

"Not very famous, I'm afraid, my boy. I was a surgeon at one of the hospitals; but I had to come West for my health. I haven't practised for over four years. That arm of yours, though, is all right. Move it around more, why don't you? I had a good look at it while you were out—"

But Misery's sudden whoop cut him off. Incredulously, he was making fancy flourishes with his right arm and hand; and abruptly he dashed back the covers and jumped right out of bed.

"Whoopee ti-yi-yo!" he howled, and did a quick crow hop. "Mister Crawford, suh, you are a wonder!" he declared, grabbing the doctors's hand and shaking it with gusto. "I never expected to ever git another job o' work out of that hand, an' here it is a'most as good as new again! *An',*" he added, turning that right hand over and over as though he would never be done marvelling at it, "there ain't any sign of a cut!"

Crawford chuckled in his quiet, droll way.

"No," he said. "I didn't have to do any cutting. Just a case of ligament adjustment and—"

"Never mind the fancy names, Doc—jest tell me what in heck ailed it."

"Why, not a great deal. The arm was wrenched pretty badly; in fact, I was rather astonished not to find your shoulder dislocated also. There was a twisted ligament, a number of—"

"Well," Misery declared, "I never would of believed it possible I'd be usin' that hand again without some drastic things bein' done. Er—while Taisy's out of the house for a bit, would you mind huntin' 'round fo' that short gun I was packin' when I come here?"

"That .44 with the sawed-off barrel?"

"That's the baby."

Doc Crawford frowned. He looked at Misery dubiously, cleared his throat a couple of times and finally said:

"I kind of feel some way like, mebbe, I'd be doing you a disservice to comply with that request, son."

"Now don't you go to worryin' about that, suh. I been weaned a week or two an' figure on bein' big enough to take care o' myself—"

"You haven't done extremely well at it so far," said the doctor mildly.

Misery scowled.

"Luck has been ag'in me," he muttered darkly; "but I got 'er all chalked up, an' my number's on the ball this time—yes, *suh!* As that varmint Curly Bill would say, 'You watch my smoke!' If I don't nail that lobo's hide to the fence an' square things up with that double dealin' Dude, then my name ain't Misery Jones Fenner!"

Chapter 15

Morgan Crawford shook his head.

"It is all right to brag, my boy, if you're inclined that way, but bragging and doing are more often than not two entirely different things. And, as my daughter is fond of saying, 'Two wrongs never make a right'—"

"Mebbe not," Misery muttered. "But I ain't one to be pushed around. I'm peaceful

as cloves on a Christmas ham so long as I'm
treated Christian—I can be sociable as a bartender to a sheriff; but when these tinhorns
starts shovin' me round it's time for the in-
nercent bystanders to start huntin' holes in
a hurry! 'Live an' let live' is my motto—but
just keep the price down in reason."

What Morgan Crawford might have said
to that has never been unravelled, because
there came a knock just then and the kitchen
door opened and Short Beer Ballard stepped
gingerly in and pulled off his hat with a:

"Howdy, gents."

Misery eyed him uncharitably.

"I thought you'd gone back to rustlin'
steers."

"Now is that kind—I ask yuh?" Ballard
looked to Crawford appealingly. "Here I've
done rode all of these miles to do him a
Christian service an' all he's got to say to
me is: 'I thought you'd gone back to rustlin'
steers!' Virtue sure is its own reward, an'
danged pore return for the trouble!"

Ballard wiped the sweat off his freckled
face and filled his jowls with a whittled-off
chew. Then he said to Crawford soberly:

"How is he, Doc? Reckon he could make
out to ride for a spell—"

"Absolutely not," Crawford said. "He's

got no business on his feet right now—look how excitement has flushed his face. He shouldn't be up before tomorrow, and I could not advise riding before another whole week."

" 'S too bad," sighed Ballard, shaking his head. "What kind of flowers do you favour, boy? Do you want any extry trimmin's?"

"What are you talkin' about?" growled Misery, scowling.

"I'm talkin' about your end, that's what! Do you want I sh'd send fer a sky-pilot or do you reckon to make port unshrived?"

Crawford eyed the fat man worriedly. "Are we to infer—?"

"I ain't never met that guy, Mister; but Curly Bill's got the same hunch I had an' he's headed this direction hellity-larrup— an' what I mean, he ain't slickin' leather for the exercise! Ike Clanton's with him, an' Jaw Bone Clark, an' Jim Wolf an' Jerry Barton an' a whole pile of other tough monkeys; an' if this gent sets any store by his health he'd better dig for the tules in a hurry!"

Crawford's face got white as the bone handles of Ballard's twin six-shooters. He seemed mighty upset and fingered his necktie nervously.

"But would he dare violate—"

"Violate!" Ballard snorted. "Mister, Bill Graham would violate *anything!* Ain't you heard what happened in town yesterday?"

"What was that?" asked Misery, reaching for his clothes.

"Well, it wasn't real serious," Ballard sniffed, "but it mighta been—an' it all comes out of you puttin' crazy notions in people's heads. Judge Burnett was some impressed with that re-form line you was passin' out the other day. Special that part about him holdin' camp meetin's till they got a reg'lar preacher in town. Yesterday he undertook to see how many brands he could save from the burnin'. He opened up in Babcock's bar, an' you ort to see the crowd he got—every squirt an' his uncle was there. An' just when things was gettin' earnest an' Jack Schwartz was fixin' to pass the hat around, in comes Curly Bill, an' Ike Clanton right along with 'im!

"Judge had moved Nick's tables all back an' fixed all the chairs in rows. There was two vacant seats right next to the bar, an' Bill an' Clanton took 'em. They hadn't hardly got seated when several of the boys near the back slipped out. The rest was danged quick to foller suit. Inside two minutes the Judge didn't hev no congregation at all

159

but Graham an' that crazy Ike Clanton. When the sounds of that exodus quieted down, Curly Bill looks the Judge right square in the eye an' he says, 'Come back here, Reverend! We've done took chips in this game an' we aims to see the deal through.'

"The Judge he squirmed around some, but Curly Bill was real firm. 'Me an' Ike,' he says, 'was feelin' real low an' we allowed we'd come in an' mebbe yore sermon would cheer us up some. Seems like the rest of yore flock has done sneaked out, but you go right ahead an' orate, friend, or hell is due to pop any minute.' An' he made a few passes with his smoke-pole so's to centre the Judge's attention.

"Well, the Judge seen he was in for it then, so he pitched right in an' flipped off a real fine sermon. I was standin' outside the window, an' I want to tell you the smell of brimstone was somethin' fierce; an the Judge sure laid it on to them. I guess he figured he was a goner anyhow an' might as well speak his mind. Which he shore done. Then he says, 'If the congregation will now arise I will pronounce the partin' benediction."

"But Curly Bill snaps, 'Git back ahind that bar, friend, an' don't try to skimp the fixin's.

That sermons done got me an' Ike millin' 'round an' sure-enough pointed for glory— but we ain't saved yet, by any means. We're allowin', however, a good rousin hymn might shove us into the gospel corral. Git tuned up an' hop into it!"

"Well, them two varmints liked the Judge's singin' so well they kep' him at it for an hour or more. Then Bill says, grinnin', 'You done give us a pretty fair show, friend. Ef me an' Ike ain't got religion now, it shore ain't no fault of yorn. Seein's how yo' throat must be feelin' tolerable dry, we'd feel plumb pleased to hev you step down to Schwartz's bar with us. The likker will be on me.' "

For a couple of moments there was nothing more said; then Short Beer declared:

"The Judge was right lucky, but if Curly Bill catches up with you, your headstone's goin' to read some different. Come on, boy—grab yo' hat an' let's start siftin'."

"In a minute," Misery growled. "Recollect that I'm a invalid an' all this rushin' ain't good for me. Where-at's my short-barrelled six-gun, Doc?"

Crawford got it from the sideboard drawer, and Misery tucked it in the waistband of his trousers, underneath the flaps of his vest. Then he buckled his gunbelt on and said:

161

"I wonder could I borry yo' hat, Mister Crawford, suh? Might get sunstruck was I to ride without one."

Crawford loaned him his black derby.

Then Misery shook his hand and said:

"You've been a good friend to me, Doc, an' I'll sure be rememberin' it. Wherever I roam I will always treasure the golden hours I've spent with you here alongside the Galeyville trail. An' some day, suh, when I'm reinstated as my father's own true son—"

But he choked up there and could say no more. He gave Crawford's hand a final squeeze and looked around for Taisy.

Taisy was still out doing the chores, and Ballard was in a great sweat to be gone. Then Jones remembered that he hadn't any horse; but Ballard said:

"Never mind that. I've done brought one along for you—a big one with plenty of bottom. An' you're sure goin' to need it, because Curly Bill's all done with fooling!"

Chapter 16

Curly Bill would get them if he could—that much went without saying. There was one other fact that could be taken for granted: he would hang on to their trail till hell froze, and then skate after them over the ice.

"You wait an' see," declared Ballard dourly; "the woman scorned is a plain rag doll alongside of Curly Bill!"

Within the hour it began to look as though Short Beer were right. The long reaches of the San Simon Valley looked jumbled enough to hide out an army. Yet when they abruptly swung left from the trail on the short cut to Tanque and Solomonsville, a column of smoke announced their intentions; and when Short Beer, swearing, made to shift into Whitlock Valley, three shafts of blue-grey curling smoke showed above the Peloncillo Mountains.

Short Beer pulled up disgusted.

"King Bill has done sent the word out, boy. I reckon they've done spiked your las' chance now. It's root hog or die—"

"Root hell!" snarled Misery, and cut a line west toward Bowie. Ballard, using quirt and spur, sent his grey bronc pelting after him. But almost at once a new smoke showed. Thin and straight as an arrow, it cleaved the metallic sky above Dos Cabezas Mountains, and Short Beer shook his head.

"We might's well throw in the sponge," he sighed. "This here is Bill Graham's stompin' ground. We ain't got a chance of—"

But Misery Jones wasn't listening. He was off again with the speed of a dust devil, headed for the Pinalenos.

"Great sakes!" Ballard shouted. "Ain't no use headin' up in there. That's Curly Bill's hip-pocket, boy! Might's well quit an' be done with it as to go whamming up into *them* hills!"

Yet Misery paid no attention—not even when another new smoke shook its lazy spirals above the slashed ridges. Though he pulled his horse down to a walk then, and with a scowl yanked out his rifle.

"You ain't figurin' to swap lead with 'em, be you?" Short Beer licked his lips nervously.

"I—" Misery began, and then shut his teeth hard down on it.

For a sudden idea had come to him, and he slammed his bronc around on the back-trail. Ballard's three chins bounced like Misery's borrowed derby as they went galloping hellity-larrup across the grease-wood flats and cat-claw hollows, bending back again toward the San Simon.

"I hope you know what you're doin', hombre," Ballard wheezed as he spurred to keep up. "Where in blue blazes you goin'?"

"The Flystroms' claimshack—"

Ballard heaved out a dismal groan as though the worst of his fears were confirmed.

"Hev you gone plumb daffy? Curly Bill's found out how you fooled him out there."

"Oh, he has, eh?" With hardly a pause Misery sawed his horse left till its head pointed straight toward Dude Fenner's. "All right," he snarled; "we'll go to the Broken Bow then."

"Out of the whale's mouth into the lion's! Ain't I told you more'n forty-five times the Dude's hand in glove with them owl-hooters?"

"He won't be, time I get done with him!"

Ballard's eyes rolled like a Mexican's.

"Won't you never git it through your head? The Dude's a'most as bad as Bill Graham! He don't spit less'n Curly Bill tells him!"

Ballard quit talking sudden-like and wildly sawed on his reins. He threw his big grey away back on its haunches, for Jones had stopped square across the trail, and the light of his eyes was plain ugly.

"What's that?" he demanded. "Say that again!"

"I said the Dude—"

"Then, by grab, you're a liar! The Dude ain't no polish to the Fenner name; but no Fenner—not even the Dude—could be such a belly-crawlin' black-guard, suh, as to boot lick fo' a mealy-mouth outlaw!"

Ballard quailed from Misery's look; but he stuck right to his statement doggedly.

"That Dude is a dang sidewinder," he muttered. "You don't hev to take my word for it—mebbe you can pry the truth out of Hawswell. They're all in it together, boy. Curly Bill, Dude an' Jess Hawswell—they're all out t' do ol' man Fenner out of that ranch; an' believe me, they're sure goin' to get it!"

Misery reached across and caught Ballard's shoulder, into which his fingers bit like a wolf trap.

"Listen!" he said. "I'm, a Fenner—*see?* I'm a Fenner myself an' I don't stand fo' that kinda yap outa no one! I can believe what you say about Hawgswill; but the Dude is my brother—"

"I don't give a rip if he's Saint Pete's brother! You'll—*Look out!* Here they come!"

Misery's quick look proved Short Beer right. Out of the cat-claw and juniper tore a ragged line of lowriding horsemen, waving rifles and howling like Indians. It was some of Graham's bunch; for there, in the lead, rode Barton and Jaw Bone, and the bullets began flying like hailstones.

There was not one chance in ten thousand that Ballard and Misery could hold that crowd off, and Ballard, for one, wasn't trying. He had whirled his horse and was pelting like mad for the mouth of a draw just beyond the last ridge; with a curse Misery Jones tore after him.

They made it somehow, though Misery lost Crawford's derby and Ballard's horse threw a hind shoe. But this was no time for picking up parts, and they pushed both their broncs to the limit. Luckily for them, it was late afternoon and the shadows of evening were gathering. Hell-bent down the draw they rode, dodging the boulders and ripping through the gnarled mesquites with scant regard for their slashing needles. They had room for just one thing in their minds—that was to get out of reach of Graham's rifles.

It was a tumbled region through which they rode, a place of high crags and deep gullies; and each time a canyon opened off the draw they took a different direction.

The swirling shadows were grown thick as

smoke when Ballard finally reined in his horse and sat, with head canted, listening.

"I guess we've done shook 'em," he wheezed at last, and mopped his streaked face with a shirt sleeve. He looked at Misery reproachfully. "You sure ort to advertise in the papers, boy—you certain sure ort to. You've got them there reducin' pills beat forty-six ways from the joker. I ain't knowed you hardly ten days an' I've lost twenty pounds a'ready!"

"Quit worryin' about your leaf lard an' focus yo' mind on this lan'scape. Where in hell are we?"

Ballard shook his head.

"All I know for certain is I never been here before," he grunted, and wiped his sweating face again. "Whew! Slit my sides an' call me tow sack!"

"Tow sack's good for somethin'," Jones said, and turned his bronc up the foot-slopes. "Come on, let's get out of these bottoms an' find where we are."

"If you got to know, we're in the San Simon—"

"Good!" Jones said. "We'll strike for the Fenners'—"

"That's the first place Graham 'll hunt us when his scouts send word they've lost us!"

But Misery kept on riding. With an exasperated grunt Ballard swung his own bronc after him.

The slope they were climbing led to a ridge; they could see its hog bulk crouched against the black sky, and Short Beer kept muttering under his breath as he urged his tired horse after Misery's. There were no stars showing, and the slope was a mass of piled shadows.

"Fella 'd think you goin' to a fire!" Ballard growled, at last catching up with him. "What's all the tarnashun hurry?"

"Mebbe it *is* a fire," Misery muttered; and Short Beer, staring where he pointed, saw a lighter patch in the night's dark black. He pulled rein, fingering his six-guns.

Misery, too, had stopped his horse. He sat silent, with a knee hooked round the horn, morosely peering into the night.

"It might be a campfire," Ballard said; but Misery doused that hope on the instant.

"That's no campfire." He had his head up, sniffing. "I smell burnin' cloth—that's a shack afire! C'mon—"

"Hey—wait!" cried Ballard, grabbing his breath. "Criminy Christmas an' hellity-larrup! By grab, I think I know where—"

"Wheah are we then?"

"If it's where I think," Ballard grumbled, "we better be turnin' back pronto. I got a mighty oncomfortable feelin'," he said, "that we're on that ridge out back of the Flystroms' claimshack!"

Chapter 17

They were.

It was apparent the moment Misery crested the ridge and peered down into the firelit hollow that had once been the Flystroms' ranch yard. As soon as his hunch had been thus confirmed, Short Beer Ballard was all for taking a long pear in some other direction; but Misery had different notions.

The Flystrom yard was filled with horsemen; and over by the backhouse, away from the flames of the burning claimshack, they saw Julie struggling with a couple of Curly Bill's men. Other Curly Bill riders were looting the sheds and outbuildings.

Misery swung silently out of his saddle—not that there was any great need of hush-hush tactics on the two friends' part. Graham's owl-hoot riders were whooping up the night with oaths and wild laughter, interspersed with sly quips and bawdy humour tossed dogbone-fashion at the subdued Julie.

Jones could see the scornful curl of her lips, and his own mouth tightened in silent admiration of the pluck that buoyed her up against life's bitter buffets. She had lost her mother and, through the Dude's shenanigans, her reputation; and now, while most girls would have wailed to high heaven, there she stood with her head thrown back and watched these vandals burn her home. And never a whimper, never a sign that there went her last hopes in sparks and ashes.

Jones got down out of his saddle grimly, and Ballard, scowling, followed his lead. They dropped to the ground and squirmed on their bellies to where, from a point on the ridge's elevation, they could most fully cover the scene below.

Misery parted the wind-stirred grass with his rifle. His narrowed glance was bright as a knife-blade as he eyed the two men holding Julie. A sudden flare from falling roof timbers sent a wild swirl of sparks shearing into the night; and at that moment he squeezed the trigger.

The nearest man let go of Julie and clutched at his chest with both clawed hands. Through the roar of the flames his shriek was heard; and the milling horsemen larruping round him turned quick looks that were just in time to see the fellow on Julie's left go reeling drunkenly into the back-house as Ballard's Sharps boomed out like a cannon.

Graham's men, caught flat in the bright stab of flames from the burning buildings, stood petrified for some seconds while a third man dropped among the held horses that went straightway up on their hind legs into the air with shrill screams and snortings. Then three of them broke pell-mell for the timber, their reins ripping out of the horse-guard's hands. He let out a yell, and the rest of Graham's gang let loose of their plunder and dived for their saddles, only one or two pausing to slam a few slugs at the night's hemming black.

Jaw Bone's shout sailed up like a rocket.

"Gawd, boys!" he cried. "It's the *Earps!* Hit leather!"

Ballard's next shot knocked the hat off his head; and Misery, triggering madly, drove a hole between Gila Jack's popping eyes and knocked another man out of his saddle.

The firelit clearing fairly shrilled with lead, and all was shouts and confusion and pitching horses, with swearing riders trying to get into saddles that heaved and shied like a platter of jelly. And over all roared the pounding boom of Short Beer's Sharps and the crack!-crack!-crack! of Misery's rifle.

By the door of the harness-shed one man crouched and flung quick shots at the flash of their rifles. By the sagging corral two more worked triggers—cool hands, these, who were not to be spooked into making fool plays.

A geyser of dirt pelted Misery's face. As he reared back, blinded, a pair of blue whistlers ripped the flaps of his vest. Then he was hugging the ground again, pawing his eyes clear and spitting the grit from his stinging lips.

The man by the harness-shed took sudden courage. He leaned clear out from his covert. Ballard's Sharps boomed an answer, and the man collapsed like a balloon.

Misery crammed his Winchester with the last of his cartridges and drove white flame at the corral-screened pair. One man rose, spinning, and suddenly wilted across the peeled poles.

And then, in a flash, the clearing was emptied, the outlaws gone in the hoof-churned dust.

"Just the way," Ballard grunted derisively, "we chased the damn Yanks off'n Mission-ary Ridge that time I was Brevet-Major with General Bragg! Criminy Christmas! You should of seen them bluecoats curl their tails."

"I should of liked to," Jones said dryly. "Matter of fact, it was the other way 'round—that's where I got my hand stove up. Now leave off the bull-throwing an' go catch up yo' horse. Miz' Julie's gone, an' we better be huntin' her—I hope to hell she ain't been shot."

"Amen to that," Ballard muttered queerly, and Misery shot a quick look at him, won-dering, for there'd been a husky something in the fat man's tone that was foreign to it, tight-choked with worry.

Then they were pounding downslope, ri-ding into the clearing where the fitful glow from the smouldering embers was all that was left of the Flystroms' claim-shack. They searched around till long after daylight, but without finding Julie or a clue to her fate. She was gone—vanished completely.

It was seven-fifteen and getting hot when Misery and Short Beer, unshaved and trailbegrimed, looked down on the headquarters buildings of Broken Bow Ranch. The place looked calm and peaceful as a pink-ribboned kitten lapping up milk; but Misery was not deceived.

"They may be heah, or they may not," he said; "but we better find out before we stick our chins out. This may be a trap. Stay heah with the broncs while I scout things out."

"They? Who you talkin' about now? Them Fenners?"

"Curly Bill an' his vinegaroons," Misery said harshly. "They've had time by now to know it wasn't the Earps that shot 'em up last night. Curly Bill's a slick one. If he's snagged on to Julie—"

"You hold the horses, boy—*I'll* do the lookin'," Ballard said, and there was bell-metal in the tight sound of his voice.

But Misery was already working his way down the slope and, with a muttered oath, Ballard stayed with the ponies; but his pale eyes raked the yard below with a promise borne out by his lifted rifle.

After a while there came a low whistle and looking, he saw Misery beckoning him down.

When he came up with the horses, Misery said:

"They're not here. I've quartered the place pretty careful. So far's I can see, there ain't nobody here but Old Joe Fenner, the cook, an' a soldierin' puncher that's mendin' a saddle out back of the corral."

"What you aim to do?"

"I'm goin' to talk to old Joe."

"Goin' to try to convince him you're a Fenner?"

"I'm goin' to try," Misery said, but without much conviction. "Mostly, though, what I'm after is a line on the Dude. He's goin' to mend his pilferin' ways danged quick or I'm—"

"You can't make a silk purse out of a sow's ear," said Short Beer gruffly. "The on'y thing that'll cure that sidewinder is a dose of hot lead."

Misery's look came around bright and hard.

"You keep yo' gun off the Dude—d' you heah me? He may be forty kinds of a skunk, but he's still my brother an' I won't have him shot."

"Shootin's too good fer him," scowled Short Beer darkly, and fingered the rope that was coiled on his saddle.

"Never mind," Misery grunted. "You leave him to me."

They rode up to the steps of the ranch house veranda, and Misery called out a greeting.

"Keep yo' eye skinned on that saddle-mendin' gopher over there by the corral," he told Ballard. "I ain't cravin' no shot in the back."

Then the screen door opened and old Joe Fenner stood there eyeing them, with his gnarled hands clamped about the head of his cane.

"Howdy, suh," Misery said. "If the Dude is around I would like to see him."

Old Joe's frame stiffened and his head tipped forward and he peered at Misery with his pale, rheumy eyes.

"So it's *you* back again." The words were blunt, harshly grating. "Well, you've wasted your time. He's not around here." His stare turned dour, and he said uncharitably, "Turn them horses around an' get off my ranch."

That was not like old Joe. In the old days he had been a model of courtesy and had fed more tramps and drifters than there were folks in this Territory.

Misery looked at him, startled.

"Why, suh—" he began.

The old man lifted his cane in a curt gesture.

"Go!" he said. "Turn your horses and go before I forget myself and bring shame to the Fenner name!"

Misery stared at his father, bewildered. He could not believe his ears; could not believe that this was old Joe talking, ordering people off of his ranch. In the old days his Dad would have been shocked at the thought of it—horrified. Yet there he stood, bitterly ordering them off.

It was Ballard who found his voice first. The fat man hooked a chubby knee around the horn and got out the makings while he looked old Joe over coldly.

"Kinda seems," he said, "like you ort to be told things, Mister. I don't know you from Adam's off-ox—nor you me. But it's a damn funny father who will turn his own son away from the gate. I'm su'prised at you, sir—su'prised to know that there are such folks." He turned on the old man with withering scorn.

Misery was opening his mouth to protest, but Short Beer said gruffly:

"Hobble your lip, boy. I'm talkin'. It's high time this old fool was bein' told a thing or two what all the country knows but him. The simplest soul in these mountains knows Dude Fenner for a crook—an' a connivin', obstreperous scoundrel to boot! An' here you been coddlin' him long as you've been here," he told old Joe grimly. "Nursin' the viper that's been sellin' you out—"

"Enough!" shouted old Joe, voice shaking with outrage. "I won't hear your lies—*I won't!* Get off my ranch!"

"Oho!" Ballard scowled. "So it's lies, is it? Well, you can hev it that way if you want it; but if I had a spread as fine as this an' it was *my* son that was sellin' me out for a miserable handful of silver, I'd make out to *do* somethin' about it!"

The old man stared at them, and the hands that gripped his cane were shaking as with a palsy. Again Misery would have interfered, but Short Beer wouldn't let him.

"Some people," he said, "has got no more sense than a little babe what ain't been weaned yet—they wouldn't know enough to get out of the rain. Anyone that wouldn't know his own son, by grab, wouldn't know lead if it popped them in the eye!"

"You can't talk to my father like that! Hell's whiplash!" shouted Misery, catching hold of Ballard's shoulder; but Short Beer shook him off.

He growled, leaning forward to eye Fenner sharply.

"This precious Dude you're so damn' fond of has been gamblin' for months in Nick Babcock's bar—throwin' your place away hand over fist! Him an'—

"That's a bare-faced lie!" Fenner shouted. "He couldn't have been because he doesn't own it. Broken Bow ranch—"

"Is recorded in *your* name—sure!" Ballard sneered. "An' willed to Dude Fenner— which is what he's been gamblin' on, as everyone knows. Promissory notes! Curly Bill's got enough right now to take this place out from under your nose!"

Old Joe went back a pace, looking startled. But his faith was great. He had put his trust in the Dude's integrity; he would not let any man undermine it. His thoughts showed plainly on his wrinkled face; and then a great wrath showed plainly there, too. With the skin of his cheeks gone pink and mottled, he said in a tightchoked, husky voice:

"Get off of this ranch! Get off of it—both of you! Go, before I do you a hurt!"

What thoughts his words stirred in Misery's head were not disclosed; but his shoulders drooped and his soul looked sick; and Ballard, noticing, snarled:

"By criminy! Graham will take your shirt! An', by the Almighty, you shore deserve it!"

Misery straightened suddenly with lifted hand. Ballard heard the hoof pound, and whirled a look.

"It's the Doc!" he growled, and turned back to Fenner.

Sore troubled as Misery was, he kept watching. His uneasiness heightened as the Doc drew nearer. And then Morgan Crawford stopped at the edge of the porch. His clothes were torn and his face was brush-clawed; lather lay like soap along his horse's flanks.

"Jones!" he cried, his voice choked with anguish. "Thank God I've found you! Curly Bill's gang—*they've carried off Taisy!*"

Chapter 18

The bitter details were quickly told. At the dawn's first light the outlaws had come rampaging down on the Crawford claimshack with shouts and wild yells and much firing of pistols. They had hauled Morgan Crawford out of his bed and tied him up with his own belt-strap. With a peremptory oath, Graham had bidden Taisy dress and be quick about it or they'd burn the nails off her father's feet. And when at last, trembling, she had come from her room, they'd lashed her on to a horse and ridden off toward the hills.

"You tell Misery Jones I've got her," Graham snarled. "We'll *see* who's brass-collar dog around here!" And then off they'd gone in a wild spurt of dust.

Ballard's face was black with fresh hate.

"An' I guess that damn' Dude was right with 'em!" he snarled.

But old Doc Crawford shook his head. "I didn't see him—"

"Of course you didn't!" Joe Fenner bristled. "My son wouldn't be mixed up in a thing like that—they'd ought to hang those scoundrels!"

"They'll hang all right if *I* git hold of 'em!" Ballard whirled his horse to face Morgan Crawford. "Which way'd they go? Which hills did they strike for?"

But Crawford was vague. He seemed suddenly to age, and his hands started shaking. Then a hard racking cough turned his pale face purple, and he swayed in his saddle, catching its horn with both hands.

It seemed as if the group had forgotten Misery.

It was old Joe Fenner who first broke the silence.

"Where's that young fool off to?" His gnarled hand pointed its cane toward the lane.

Ballard, whirling a look, yelled: "Hold on! What're you doin'?"

But it was plain enough. Misery was stripping the gear from his loose-coupled roan. And now, with a rope, he was striding corralwards.

"Don't you dare touch those horses!" old Joe yelled wrathly.

Misery paid no attention. He slipped through the bars and soon had one snagged—a big powerful bay that promised bottom and speed.

With an oath, Ballard commenced pulling the hull from his own bronc then; and short seconds later he, too, was leading a fresh horse from the Fenner bronc pen.

"Wait fer me!" he snarled as Misery mounted.

But Misery wasn't waiting—neither for Short Beer nor for old Joe Fenner, who, cane lifted, was coming off the porch like the wrath of God.

He turned the big bay into the lane and out through the gate while Crawford, stiffly sliding from his saddle, caught old Joe's shoulder and wrested away his thick cane.

He tried to reason with the Broken Bow owner, but old Joe was beside himself. He shouted for Hawswell, his foreman—even called for the Dude; but at last, strength spent, he leaned weakly against the porch rail and dropped his arms impotently.

Crawford, eyeing him, shook his head.

"I don't know," he said grimly, "what the Dude has told you, but the truth is, Fenner, that that boy's your son. I've tended him through two bad hurts and I've heard his ravings when he was out of his head; and I'm telling you, man to man, he's a Fenner—and the only one with good sense I've met!"

Old Joe glared at him; but Crawford's opinions were not to be shaken.

"Pull yourself together, man! This is a time for thought and plenty of it. Your son, Dude, has been travelling in bad company for quite a spell. He's thicker than splatter with Curly Bill Graham, and God knows how he'll ever get out of it. I don't think he's been mixed in Graham's stage-robbing stunts or this kidnapping, but he's gambled away a small fortune to him in promissory notes secured by this ranch."

He looked old Joe straight in the eye. It was Fenner's glance that faltered. And, worried as he was about his daughter's safety,

Morgan Crawford was moved by the crushed, forlorn look of old Joe's shoulders.

He turned his glance away uncomfortably, not liking to witness the old man's hurt. When he looked again he was startled by the change in old Fenner's features. A cold wrath had replaced old Joe's disillusionment; his eyes were bright with it, his whole body vibrant. Such anger was a shocking thing in a man as mild as Fenner had seemed. Crawford eyed him, startled, half alarmed by his look.

"Pull yourself together," he said again. "The Dude is a bad one, but more to be pitied than censured. He is weak—easily led—"

"He's a crookl" old Joe said fiercely. "A black-guard who would sell his own brother— a disgrace to his name! I see it all now," he muttered, passing a hand across his tired eyes. "A cheap, gambling tinhorn—"

"Whatever he is," Crawford interrupted, "your other son, Jones, is the salt of the earth. If anyone can bring a measure of happiness out of this devil's tangle, it will be him. You must pin your hopes on him, Mister Fenner—even as I do. He is a man foursquare—a man, as they say around here, to 'ride the river with'. If any power on earth can save my daughter, that power will be wielded by your son, Jones Fenner!"

Chapter 19

Misery had a forty-yard lead when they pulled out of the Broken Bow ranch yard, and not until he was getting out of his saddle in front of McConaghey's bar did Short Beer Ballard catch up with him. He gave Jones a reproachful look as he half fell out of his saddle.

"Of all the ongrateful hairpins I ever met—"

But as usual, Misery wasn't standing around to swap small-talk. He was parting the batwing doors with his shoulder, and his right hand was close to his pistol. With a grunt Ballard followed in after him.

It wasn't yet noon, and the barflies were all sawing wood in the alleys. The place was deserted, but Jones tramped straight to the bar and banged on its top with a bottle. With a couple of groans and a yawn that showed all his gold teeth and his tonsils, a barman stood up from broaching a barrel and regarded Jones with a jaundiced stare.

"My Gawd," he said. "Are you back again?"

"Never mind that," growled Misery. "Where's that damn Curly Bill hiding out at?"

The barkeeper shut his dropped jaw with a snap and, grabbing a towel, began polishing glasses as if Misery weren't even around the place. But Misery wasn't any kind of man to ignore. He reached across the bar and fastened a grip on the barkeep's collar and twisted till the man's eyes bulged. He said:

"I wa'n't talkin' to heah my head rattle!"

"I—I thought you was talkin' to that fat fella with you—"

"Ever heah what thought did to the cat?" Misery's look was dark and foreboding. —The barman's belligerence vanished. "I— I ain't seen Graham since yesterday—"

Misery turned on his spurs and clanked outside and rode forthwith to Jack Dall's saloon, where he left his bronc at the tie rail.

"Somethin'," Ballard wheezed, "is bound t' give if this keeps up much longer. Either the seat o' my pants or the saddle, one or t'other."

But Misery never even glanced at him. There was a cold bleak look in the slant of his eye, and the jut of his jaw promised violence. He parted Dall's batwings and stopped squarely in them while a cold smile quirked his beard-bristled face.

"Hello, there, John," he said very softly, "I guess you'll do till Graham comes along. One polecat smells as bad as another. Get out of that gun-belt—*pronto!*"

Three men had been lounging beside Dall's bar. The middle one had whirled clear around at Misery's first words. He now stood crouched there, pale and stiff, a half pace aside from his two companions. A reaching hand had stopped within an inch of his gun. His black, scowling stare showed a lust to grab it, but his twitching fingers betrayed reluctance; and Ballard cursed when he saw who it was.

"Go on!" Misery drawled. "Peel out of that gun-belt."

Perhaps it was the slow casualness of Misery's order that deceived the Dude. At any rate he made no move to get rid of his arsenal; and while his hand did not close on the gun so near it, his red lips curled with an open contempt.

"Since when has a Fenner taken orders from a range tramp? Go on, you skunk. Get back in the alley with the rest of the drunks."

Misery grinned, very thinly, very full of menace.

"I ain't drunk *this* time—so don't try to roll me like you did before."

Colour flagged the Dude's lean cheeks; and one of the tinhorns with him said: "Gosh! I wouldn't take that talk off my ol' man even."

The Dude's reaching hand closed tight around his gun, and his cheeks turned ugly as he started forward.

"*I'll* take care o' him!" Ballard breathed.

But though his left arm was bulky in its swath of bandage and the whole town knew his right hand was useless, Misery held his place like the Rock of Ages; and Ballard, perforce, could not get past.

It looked for a minute as though the Dude meant business, but something abruptly slowed him down, and he stopped with a good six feet between himself and Jones. Perhaps it was something he read in Misery's face; whatever it was, his own cheeks blanched and the hand on his gun went stiff as cordwood.

"Go on—drag it," Misery taunted. 'That's your style, ain't it? Pickin' on sick fellers, widders an' orphans. What're you waitin' on—help from your side-kicks'"

"I've stood all your lip I've a mind to—"

"Did you say 'mind'?" Misery scoffed.

189

"What you use for a mind a cow wouldn't snort for! Don't make us boys laugh!"

The Dude's trembling hand half jerked out his pistol; but Misery's cold sneer cut the movement short.

"You fish-bellied shorthorn—go on an' drag it! What's holdin' you? Feel the need of Ike Clanton, or Curly Bill, mebbe? *They* won't help you—they're huntin' holes, too! Pah!" Misery snarled. "You ain't got the guts of a sick jack-rabbit!"

The Dude's face was purple, his mottled cheeks bloated. All his fine pride and tough reputation was being kicked through the mud. There were men watching who wondered why he didn't drag out his gun and shoot the socks off this stranger—but not for a million would the Dude have hauled iron and taken his chance with the man he'd defrauded. He spluttered and gurgled—looked so mad he could cry.

"It's hard to believe you're a Fenner," Jones said; then he started forward, and the Dude cringed back like a yellow cur. He bleated like a frightened sheep when Jones' right hand grabbed a hold on his shoulder. Misery's bandaged left hauled up a chair.

In a twinkling, seemed like, he was settled

in it with the squirming dandy face down in his lap. The only sound in that whole shocked bar was what lifted dust from the doeskin pants—just that, and the Dude's loud bellows.

As the barkeep later told all and sundry:

"It was funny as hell, but nobody laffed. Guess we was too embarrassed to see a growed man spanked. But spanked the Dude was—an' spanked right proper!"

Misery got up finally and dumped the Dude on the floor.

"I hope," he said grimly, "that'll be a lesson. But long as you insist on actin' like a danged spoiled brat you'll git treated like one. You ain't *bad!* You're jest mean an' ornery. It takes real guts to go hawg wild—guts an' a backbone, Johnny. All you got is a wishbone.

"Now I'm goin' to give you some good advice. You go along home an' tell old Joe Fenner you been wrong all along—you been follerin' false idols an' are goin' to *mend* yo' ways. An' see that you mend em, or you'll catch more of the same. An' just fo' a starter better git yo'self shucked of that potato-bug plumage. There ain't *nobody*, hardly, could act like a man togged out in that kind of get-up."

Without further words he turned square around and tramped toward the batwings where Ballard still stood with a hand on his six-gun. Short Beer did not turn nor move aside at once. He stood there with his fat face scowling. Then suddenly, with a snort, he turned and strode out.

Chapter 20

"Him bein' your brother kinda cramped your style, didn't it?" he said sourly, as they unwrapped their reins from the hitch-rack. "If it had been *me*, I'd sure of give him enough hot lead to bog a six-horse hitch down. Had'a damn good notion to, anyhow."

But, again, Misery paid no attention to Short Beer's disgruntled mutterings. As usual, Jones was going about his business, and that business just now was turning his bronc's face directly toward the sole building on the opposite side of the street, Nick Babcock's bar, that was backed right up to the mesa's edge where it dropped to the Turkey Creek bottoms.

And his face was set, jaw hard-clamped with determination. If he was counting the cost of what he planned, that fact was not revealed. Short Beer, eyeing him, saw only a mighty purpose in the forward swing of his shoulders as their horses plodded through the street's hock-deep dust on a line whose end was the batwing doors of Babcock's bar, headquarters of Curly Bill Graham.

"You think he'll be there?"

Misery's answer was a cold, brief nod. His narrowed eyes clung tight to the batwings, and in their depths lurked a fiercening gleam that assured there was going to be blood spilled.

"We'd ort to slip up more careful-like," Ballard muttered nervously. "Be jest like that ory-eyed gopher to gun us from a winder or somethin'—"

"Not this time," Misery told him. "There's too many people knows what's up 'round here. He'd lose face if he run any sandy like that. Nope," he said, still watching the doors, "he'll not shoot till we step inside."

"We'll be just as dead when he cracks down, though."

"You don't have to trail along. You can go set down in the shade some place an' wait until it's over."

"Hell! What you take me for?"

"Well, it's my fuss, after all," Misery said. "You don't need—"

"Humph!" Ballard snorted; then suddenly cried, "Hold on! Here comes a fella—"

It was Judge Burnett. He had just stepped off Shotwell's porch and was quartering over to intercept them.

Misery waved him away, but the Judge came on. He had his shotgun snugly under his arm, and there were rivers of sweat on his scowling face.

"Dang ye! Wait!" he yelled; and came panting up as if he were being slighted.

"Didn't ye hear me holler?" he muttered, dragging a sleeve across his red cheeks.

Still watching Babcock's, Misery said:

"You better haul off. There's like to be trouble."

"I know all about your trouble. D'ye think I been Judge of this place all these months without knowin' what's goin' on around yere? They're all in Babcock's layin' for ye—layin' for ye—Curly Bill an' the four tough bucks who rode in with 'im. *An'* them girls—"

"That's all we want t' know," Ballard growled. "Now clear outa the way. You're impedin' progress."

The Judge scowled up at them without much favour.

"Not enough sense to pound nails in a snowbank! Didn't ye hear me say they was layin' for ye?"

"Let 'em lay," Short Beer snorted. "We're goin' to knock them lobos hell west an' crooked! We're goin' to knock 'em so far it'll take a bloodhound a week t' git so much as a sniff of 'em! We ain't escaired of them shorthorns!"

"But it's a trap—"

"That's all right," Misery murmured, impatient. "We're sure obliged to you, Judge; but we knew all that 'fo' we come heah. Curly Bill's hooked them girls deliberate to fetch us in heah—we savvy that. We don't want him to feel let down. So if you'll just step out of the way—"

With a snort old Burnett stepped from their path. Then, shoving fresh shells in his shot gun, still scowling, he strode along after them.

At Babcock's hitch-rack the pair swung down and looped their reins across the peeled pole. Then Misery shifted his holster around to his left hip so that his pistol was sheathed butt forward. This gave the impression, since his left arm was bulkily swathed to the wrist in bandages, that he intended in the event of trouble to make a cross-arm draw. He would have to get that pistol out; and back of Nick's window Hawswell chuckled, and his lips drew down in a cold thin sneer. For he knew what all of Galeyville knew—that Misery's right arm was useless.

And Ballard knew that, too; and he looked at Misery dubiously.

"Don't you reckon you better let me—" Short Beer chopped off his talk with a muttered oath, for Misery was parting the batwings.

But he hadn't taken six steps inside the place, with Ballard and Burnett right back of him, when he stopped. The sides of the rooms were packed with men, miners and gamblers, with a few painted faces peering over their shoulders, and with here and there the view blocked out by the tall widebrimmed hat of a cowpoke. They were all watching breathlessly for the fun to commence, and directly before him with his back to the bar, stood Jesse Hawswell, grinning.

"And where is that fine-feathered Curly Bill Graham?" Jones demanded, blackly raking the mob with his glance. "Now I'm callin' his bluff. What's he doin'—hidin' out?

Tryin' to hunt him a fire to thaw out his feet?"

Hawswell said:

"He'll be here quick enough—just stepped out a moment to make sure the ladies is comfortable. But the time won't drag," he said with a sneer. Then the hate in him got the best of him, and he snarled at Jones Fenner gratingly, "I've a score to settle with *you*, bucko!" and splayed a quick hand by his holster.

Misery wheeled him a look with his left eyebrow raised.

"Were you makin' that music at *me*, Hawgswill?"

And Hawswell, secure in his knowledge of Misery's bum paw, said:

"Yes—*you damn' horse thief!*" and yanked out his gun in a passion.

Chapter 21

He grabbed out his gun and thumbed back its hammer; but the shot that lashed the place with a wild clamour came from the region of Misery Jones' waist. And a blue hole showed between the crooked foreman's eyes as his buckling knees sprawled him dead on the floor.

"Dead," Ballard said, "as a mackerel!"

A good many of the crowd couldn't seem to understand it; and they stared at the dead man incredulously. But a few of the crowd were peering bug-eyed at Jones, and at the short gun he gripped in his right hand—a cold, brightly glittering thing with a sawed-off barrel he had flicked from under his vest flaps. The gun on his hip was still there in its holster, but Hawswell was on the floor, dead.

Misery's eyes flashed bright as diamonds as he raked the crowd with a cold glance.

"I'm peaceful as a July zephyr, long as I'm left alone," he growled. "But tromp on my corns an' I'm a regular he-tankarora—as Hawgswill has learned to his cost. Now this pussy-footin' Curly Bill Graham has gone bull-rotten an' kidnapped a couple o' ladies—stole 'em right out of their fathers' homes without so much as a by-yo'-leave; an' that's playin' it pretty desperate. In fact, it's puttin' a rope 'round his neck. He'll be done in this country from here on out, and them as abets him will be done, too—we'll ride 'em out on a rail, by grab! There's nothin' worse," he scowled at them fiercely, "then stealin' a woman against her will; none but a low-down, sheep-dip eatin' sidewinder like this Curly Bill stinker would do it!"

There were scowls and growls and nods of assent, and several gents fingered their weapons.

"Well," blared Misery finally, "what you goin' to do about it? You goin' to turn the skunk up or ain't you?"

Put up squarely against it that way, the crowd turned fidgety and eyed one another uneasily. Curly Bill Graham was a mighty tough monkey, and his word had been law for two years now. There were not many persons around Galeyville feeling anxious to single themselves out as men who had stood against him. Luck was too fickle a goddess, and this brash-talking stranger might not live to make good; and then where in seven hells would *they* be?

So they shuffled their feet uncomfortably and not one would meet Jones' eye.

Jones' glance marked them scornfully.

"So this heah's the tough town of Galeyville, is it? Hell's whiplash!" he snarled. "There was more salt in Lot's wife than there is in the bunch of you! What a drool-jowled bunch of sheep-killin' fisty dogs!"

And Short Beer's nod was contemptuous. "You couldn't find a gut in the bunch of 'em!" A pale-faced gambler spoke up then with a quaint and Southern dignity.

"That's as may be. But the ladies, suh, are just off the balcony—first door to the left of the stairs, suh."

Jones started forward, then as suddenly stopped, and his eye met Ballard's suspiciously. Ballard nodded.

"A plain damn' lie, if you're askin' me."

The pale-faced gambler flushed.

"Yo' pahdon, suh!" he choked, white-lipped. "Are you presuming to doubt my word, suh?"

But Misery had never been one to bandy words, and the occasion just now was urgent. "Take a look," he told Ballard softly; but before Short Beer had more than put his weight on the bottom step there came from somewhere above a swift exclamation, a woman's scream and an instant clatter of breaking glass, with, seconds later, a dull, muted thump and a crashing of brush that sent Misery charging head-long through the scattering crowd. He had no need to consult a medium to know what had happened upstairs. At the last minute Curly Bill's bravado had deserted him and he had departed, post haste through a window.

Misery smashed a slow-mover out of his

way and shoved his belt gun through one of Nick's windows that gave on the Turkey Creek bottoms. His guess had been right! There Curly Bill went, like a trainload of heifers, hellity-larrup on a long-necked black, racing toward the Sam Simon as fast as quirt and both spurs would take him. Already he was out of decent pistol range, but Misery emptied his six-shooter.

With a curse he was back through the crowd again, thumbing fresh loads in his pistols. He flipped the short gun back under his vest. He caught hold of the Judge and shoved him toward the stairs.

"You stick with the women—we'll git 'im!"

Then he dashed after Ballard and piled into his saddle. They took out in Graham's wake like a whirlwind.

Chapter 22

"He's headin' for Tombstone!" Ballard yelled. They swung their horses out of the wash and madly larruped for the ridge across which Curly Bill had just as madly fled. "He's goin' to try an' get in with some more of his gang—they're scattered from here to hell an' back!"

Misery Jones said nothing. He rode with his grim eyes fixed straight ahead, alert for tricks and suspicious of ambush. For he knew as well as any man that Curly Bill could not run off this way and ever rule again in the Cherrycows. Weak men will follow a bold, bad leader, but none will follow a scared one. What Misery did not know was that Wyatt Earp was again after Graham, and had sworn to kill him for Morgan Earp's murder. But Curly Bill knew, for his spies had told him, and he had no intention of lingering.

What he had planned in kidnapping the two girls will never be known for certain, but he'd probably some notion of ransom in mind, which Misery's prompt action had throttled. Or perhaps it was the news that Wyatt Earp was again on his trail which was making Bill rattle his hocks. At any rate, he was on his way and showed no intention of stopping.

Nor was he actually making for Tombstone, as Ballard and Misery discovered later in the day when Graham's lead and his superior pony left them little but his tracks to follow. Occasionally they saw him, briefly, far off on the flats or skylined on the rimrock; but they never saw him for long at a stretch, and always he was riding as if the devil were after him.

Four times that day he changed horses, stealing when he could not borrow them. Out of fear of reprisal, many men in that country would have given Graham all they possessed.

Misery and Short Beer clung to his trail as long as there was light to see by. After that, in the cool evening shadows, they put up at a spread in the Dragoons, a two-bit, one-horse outfit whose owner appeared badly frightened.

"Did that swine stop here?" Short Beer asked him.

"No one has stopped here for months," the man growled, and backed off when Misery looked at him.

"You're a liar!" Misery said; "we followed his tracks right in through yo' gate! Loosen up an' talk quick—where's that polecat holed up at?"

The man licked his lips. With a sullen scowl he stared at the floor.

"I don't know what you're talkin' about," he muttered; and stuck to it.

They searched his place from top to bottom—the barn and the sheds, even the cupboards. But they found no sign of Curly Bill.

When it seemed certain he hadn't stopped there, but had gone on toward the Whetstones, Short Beer creased his cheeks in a horn-pout scowl and, thrusting his face within two inches of the rancher's, growled fiercely:

"You know me, I guess—Hurricane Bill, what used to be that sneakin' devil's right bower. You know me, don't you?"

The man drew back, looking scared and mean. But he said bitterly:

"I know you"; and Short Beer chuckled sinisterly. "Good!" he said. "Remember me, then. 'Cause if I ever find you been lyin', friend, I'm comin' back after your scalp."

Next morning, with the first flush of approaching dawn, they were astride their broncs and cutting for sign. They rode in ever-widening circles till, suddenly, Ballard shouted; and Misery, riding over, saw that he'd picked up Graham's trail again.

"It sure looks," Ballard said, "like Curly's aimin' to cut stick permanent. You can tell by these tracks he ain't losin' no time." And then, a little later: "That bronc of Bill's is goin' lame. He's goin' to have to git him another one quick or him an' us is goin' to hev a reunion."

Misery said nothing till, half an hour later, Ballard, staring sharply at the trail, wrinkled up his face and grunted.

"What's the matter?" he asked then.

"Well, I'll tell you," Short Beer answered. "I thought fer a while Bill was makin' for Tombstone. Then I was sure he wasn't. When we first cut sign this mornin' I figgered he was diggin' for the tules, clearin' out, if you git what I mean—makin' for the wide an' han'some. But the way he's headed right now, it's goin' to mean trouble if we keep after him. Of course, he *might* be aimin' fer Benson. But there's one of our old hangouts this side of Saint David, an' it's dollars to doughnuts that's where the wood-chuck's headed."

Misery grunted but did not slacken his horse.

"If he goes to this hide-out," Short Beer observed, "he's like to pick himself up a few friends. Some of the gang is bound to be there."

"You can quit any time you've a mind to—"

"There you go! Harpin' on *that* again! You're worse'n ol' Gen'ral Bragg—*he* was allus makin' them kind of ongrateful remarks ever' time I opened my mouth to advise him! What I was thinkin'," Ballard added reproachfully, "was that there wasn't no use in *both* of us stickin' our chins out. I *know* that gang; you don't. I was about to mention it might be a good idee fer you to go back an' see how the girls is."

"Save up some of that tongue oil for Curly Bill when we meet him," Jones said gruffly, and spurred his horse to a faster gait.

But about ten o'clock, with the sun a copper ball in the metallic brilliance of the morning sky, Short Beer's hunch was proved a good one. Curly Bill's trail diverged in a great half circle, and when they picked it up again, the sign was much fresher and showed the tracks of eight other horses.

Short Beer grunted.

"Bad as I want that hombre's hair, I don't know but what we'd better turn back," he allowed. "This ain't goin' to be no picnic."

Misery's answer was short and pungent.

"I didn't bring this horse on no picnic." And he raked spurred heels across the pony's ribs.

Curly Bill and his reinforcements, they figured, were not much more than an hour ahead of them. And the sign showed their travel to be much more leisurely than Graham's had been riding solo. But Short

Beer was again convinced the outlaws were leaving the country.

"They're still headin' west an', less'n they're goin' to Helvetia or Greaterville up in the Santa Ritas, they must be bound for California."

The notion appeared quite plausible. Graham's bunch might he planning some deviltry in either of those booming mine towns, or, as Short Beer appeared more and more certain, they might be on their way out of the country.

It was noon when they entered San Pedro Valley. They passed a little cow-ranch a few miles later, but neither of them wasted thought on food with the outlaws' trail so fresh before them.

"We ought to be sightin' them pretty quick," Misery said.

Suddenly Short Beer raised a shout.

"There they are! Off there to the left—see the dust! They ain't ten miles ahead of us!" he growled, and put his spurs to work pronto.

The dust he had seen was drifting up out of a wash or gully, and they raced their broncs for it madly. They had to close the gap between themselves and the outlaws all they could right now; once seen, they'd get no chance to. Once seen, as Ballard took pains to mention, the chances were one hundred to one Graham would lay some kind of trap for them. So they pushed their horses to the limit.

"What kind of country is ahead up there?" Misery asked.

"Iron Springs—an' a damn good place for a ambush."

Ten minutes later Short Beer muttered:

"They sure are takin' their time, by criminy! You'd think they had the country all to themselves."

"They prob'ly don't know they're bein' followed yet."

"Well, they'll know right soon!"

But when the dust rose out of the wash, both Short Beer and Misery were startled. The group of horsemen were in plain sight, not over three miles ahead of them.

"Hell!" wheezed Ballard sourly.

"That's not Curly Bill!" Misery muttered.

"No—not by your uncle's necktie. That there's the 'Lion of Tombstone' you're lookin' at: Wyatt Earp, Esquire, in person! An' them fellers with him ain't no golrammed wallflowers! I know 'em all an' wouldn't hug one of 'em—Doc Holliday,

Warren Earp, Sherm McMasters, Texas Jack an' Johnny Johnson! Reg'lar royal flush, by grab, an' surefire death if you cross 'em. I'd go up ag'in ten Curly Bills before I'd tackle Wyatt Earp!"

They sat their saddles watching the group, which jogged leisurely on toward a motte of trees.

"We better slip back of that hogback before one of them squirts spots us," Ballard said nervously.

"What for? They ain't after us—why, Earp is boss lawman of Tombstone, ain't he?"

"Not no more, he ain't. Johnny Behan's got himself made sheriff an' he's done run them fellers out—or that's what folks is sayin' anyhow. They're apt to be on the prod, an' Earp never has felt brotherly towards me. He'll think I'm still one of Curly Bill's gang an'll prob'ly let fly quick's he sees me."

"You wait here then," Misery told him. "I'm goin' to have a talk with 'em. Might be they've seen Curly Bill."

With a growled curse, Ballard followed.

The wind was blowing from Earp's crowd to them, so the sound of their horses was not heard by the group.

"They're headed for those trees over

there," Ballard said. "That's Iron Springs. Cut right—we'll take a short cut."

They swung out of a wash and into the greasewood bordering the copse that surrounded the springs just as Earp's bunch rode into the trees. Through the willow brush and cottonwoods Misery and Ballard could see them jogging along, with back of them the far dim tracery of the Mustang Mountains, rugged and bright in the dappling sunshine.

Short Beer and Misery entered the trees from the south, planning to intercept the Tombstone riders at the springs. Through the intervening brush they caught brief flashes of the water and then, abruptly, they heard a hoarse, frantic shout. Hell broke loose on the instant.

Misery and Ballard were at the edge of the brush. Between them and the white stretch of water formed by the springs was open ground. Just beyond the water, limned stark and grim against an eroded cutbank, crouched Curly Bill and eight of his men, all madly firing at something beyond.

The something was Wyatt Earp and his party.

They had just ridden into sight. The sudden appearance of the outlaws seemed to throw them into a panic. Doc Holliday whirled his horse in the space of a hand and went tearing off at full gallop.

Ballard dragged Misery off his horse.

"For Gawd's sake—*duck!*"

Misery fought loose of the fat man's grip, got his belt gun out and was throwing down on Curly Bill when Ballard struck his barrel up. Ballard wrested the six-shooter from him.

"You crazy hairpin! You want to fetch that damn' Earp after us? Curly Bill's his meat; an' he'd trail us from hell to breakfast if you cut so much as a slice off him!"

They watched Wyatt Earp, forty feet away, get coolly out of his saddle. All his company had fled, deserting him without scruple. But Earp seemed to care nothing for that. He looped an arm through his bridle rein and lifted down his shotgun. He surveyed the outlaws in calm appraisal, appearing to think no more of odds of nine to one than he would have of entering the bars of Tombstone. Misery was itching to help him, but Ballard had a good grip now and Jones couldn't even wriggle.

There was no hurry or fuss about Wyatt Earp. He had waited a long time for this moment, and he meant to savour it fully. Outlaw lead bit all about him; bullet after bullet cut through his hat, the skirt of his coat above each holster had been shot to ribbons already, there were ragged rents along the legs of his pants, and his hat brim hung in tatters. But the Lion of Tombstone stood cool as a well chain. Of a sudden he brought his shotgun up. Then his head tipped down, and his cheek brushed the stock as he squinted along his sights. Abruptly he pulled both triggers.

Misery saw Curly Bill's big hands clench tight on his gun. Then the rifle slid from them. Graham's arms flailed out, and he gave a yell that must have gone halfway to Galeyville. Then he went down side-ways behind the bank, with his eyes rolling wildly and his handsome face gone the colour of wet ashes.

"An' that's the end of him!" Short Beer muttered vindictively.

Misery's glance was back on Earp again where he stood all alone just across the pool with outlaw lead spurting dirt all about him. Hardly three seconds had passed since Graham's crowd had opened up, yet Bill was dead and Earp's crowd was taking the out-trail hellity-larrup.

Earp's shotgun was empty, and he reached

across his saddle to get the rifle scabbarded there. But his horse commenced plunging and squealing and bucking so that he had to give it up. Still keeping hold of the rein, he jerked out one of his six-shooters and, half crouched down beside his nervous bronc, fired three times beneath the animal's neck; and only then did he look around to see what his friends were doing.

Misery saw his eyes pop out and bulge; he could guess what Earp was thinking. But the Lion of Tombstone didn't think long. Keeping his crow-hopping bronc between him and the outlaws, he commenced a pronto backing. He commenced right off, but he could not go fast; his horse was nearly unmanageable, and Curly Bill's men were firing like Indians-maddened at their leader's fate, determined to bring Earp down at all costs.

When he got a little farther off, Earp tried to mount. But his cartridge-belt had fallen over his hips, and he could not swing his legs far enough to get one of them over his saddle. He managed it finally, but when he settled, low-crouched in his hull, the entire pommel had been shot away by the cursing outlaws.

When he got in his saddle, Earp departed

at once; and two minutes later Curly Bill's crowd left, riding in the opposite direction.

"Well," Ballard said, "I guess they done took him with 'em."

The two friends had examined the scene of the fight, investigating the pool from all angles. But, dead or alive, Curly Bill was gone from man's ken, never to be seen again. Misery seemed considerably put out by it.

"Never mind," Short Beer said; "you'd of got 'im if you could. But what difference does it make who got him? The sidewinder won't bother no one again, you can take my bona-fide word fer it—Wyatt Earp don't miss with a shotgun. Not when he pulls both barrels! An' if you'd cut in on that deal the Tombstone Lion would never of forgive you; he'd of hounded you long as you live. That's one thing ol' Wyatt takes pride in— evenin' up his scores. Why, I wouldn't be in Johnny Behan's boots fer all the gold in the Cherrycows!"

Misery scowled to himself.

"Don't be a hog," Short Beer told him. "You done got Hawswell, didn't you? *I* never got what the paddy shot at! Nor never yet will," he said darkly, "if *some* guys has their way."

"Well, come on," Misery said, "let's be

gettin' back. I done left my girl in a danged saloon, which isn't fittin' for any lady. Besides, now that the Fenners is willin' to admit I got some right in their barnyard, there's a idea battin' my think-box that I want to try out on Miz' Taisy—"

"Damn' good idea," Short Beer grunted, groaning up into his saddle. "I got the same idea about Julie—"

Jones turned clear around. He said distinctly:

"I'm figuring to ask Miz' Taisy's hand in marriage."

Short Beer nodded.

"I reckoned you was. I'm goin' to pop the same thing at Julie."

Misery blinked.

"I didn't suppose you knew her that well—"

"You got a lot to learn," Ballard grunted. "If it hadn't been fer that daggone Dude we'd of been married a considerable spell by now. I reckon she fell fer his elegant shape—but it ain't goin' to happen again! From to-night on out she's goin' to be Missus Bill Ballard an' no damn' guy had better look at her twice!"

And, true to his word, Short Beer married Julie; and Taisy moved over to the Fenners'.